Beyond Isaiah

PAUL S HUGGINS

Copyright © 2012 Paul S Huggins

All rights reserved.

ISBN: 1480262234
ISBN-13: 978-1480262232

DEDICATION

To my Wife and daughters, I love you.

To Mum for all the help.

To my Brother for getting me that book.

To my Grandad, gone but not forgotten.

CONTENTS

	Acknowledgments	i
1	Jack	1
2	Randal	10
3	Simon	16
4	Meeting	21
5	Sarah	25
6	Fred	32
7	Haven	37
8	Incursion	42
9	Excursion	46
10	Diversion	50
11	Discovery	56
12	Nightshift	60
13	Visiting	64
14	Return	69
15	Restock	73
16	Impenetrable	77
17	Comfort	81
18	Frustration	84
19	Sea	88
20	Answers	92

21	Homeward	97
22	Lodgings	100
23	Arrival	106
24	Truth	109
25	Rig	113
26	North	116
27	Visitor	120
28	Horde	124
29	Later	129

ACKNOWLEDGMENTS

Matthew Darst for his unwavering support and ideas

Sean T Page for implanting his metahorde theory.

Iain McKinnon and David Moody for the inspiration they injected.

1 JACK

Jack looked at his watch for the umpteenth time. The bus was already ten minutes late. He rolled his eyes at the young woman who was also wearing a business suit standing with him under the Perspex shelter.

'Only ever happens when you're in a hurry,' he said.

She smiled and gave him a stifled laugh of agreement. It was the wrong day for his car to break down. He had a meeting with the area manager first thing and needed to meet with an important client later on to appease some problems over supply.

As sales manager he always got the awkward ones. It's not his fault supply lines were a nightmare at the moment, all imports and exports were a struggle. But as always the buck stopped with him in the company and he would graciously take the blame, that's what they paid him for.

Finally the bus pulled up to the curb and with a whoosh of air the doors clattered open. Always the gentleman he let the smartly dressed woman get on first. As she walked down the aisle to get a seat he noticed the bus was quite empty for a weekday morning. In fact traffic was almost non-existent. He briefly dwelt on the fact that if he had his car he could've really put his foot down for a change.

'Can I have a single to town centre please?'

'That'll be two fifty,' replied the gruff driver.

Jack already had the correct change rattling around in his pocket and handed the warm coins to him. A ticket immediately sprang from the machine and with a quick rip he took it and headed down the bus with a quick,

'Thank you.'

The doors slammed shut as he took his seat close to the rear of the single decker. Jack was a people watcher and secretly enjoyed the occasional foray onto public transport to fulfil his pastime.

He surveyed his fellow passengers. The woman whom he had acknowledged at the bus stop had taken a seat at the front next to a small old lady with tightly permed white hair. A couple of seats behind them sat a young man who looked like he was on his way to a job interview with ill-fitting cheap suit that he really didn't look comfortable in. He also had the obligatory mobile phone attached to his head by long strands, presumably listening to the latest garage music sensation.

On the opposite side of the bus two college girls were discussing a party they had attended with giggles and mock surprise. A few rows back from the front sat an unkempt man who just looked plain ill. He was barely awake and rocked in time with the motion of the bus. At the very front sat two old women holding shopping trolleys out in front of them chatting quietly, most likely off into town on a shopping trip or an innocent gamble at the bingo hall.

Now he had taken in the people he was travelling with he turned his gaze to the countryside passing by the window outside. It was like a Sunday. He thought that maybe the flu epidemic the news programs were rambling on about was far worse than they were reporting. He scoffed at the idea, mainly as the reporters generally played up disaster rather than play it down. Panic had been caused by far less in recent years. The newscasters only had to intimate about some shortage or other and the shelves or fuel pumps would be dry by the end of that day.

He knew it wasn't the summer holidays as his wife had to contact the school to let them know that his children were off sick just before he left. A retching sound dragged him from his thoughts and back onto the bus and his associate passengers. The rough looking guy on the opposite side now confirmed that he really was sick by throwing up onto the floor at his feet. The whole bus fell quiet as everyone looked round at him, conversations now interrupted by the event.

The smell had emanated around the cabin, and it had been disgusting. Jack wasn't squeamish as he had children and was well used to distasteful smells of bodily functions. But this odour was a mixture of bile and rotten meat. He really didn't want to know what the guy had been eating, dead rat by the stench of it.

The bus pulled up suddenly by the side of the road. They were out of the town and now headed out into the country.

'Oh great,' said Jack under his breath 'as if I wasn't late enough already.'

The driver stepped out of his compartment letting the door close with an angry clunk behind him. He strolled up the aisle and stopped at the row the man was sitting in and placed his fists on his hips.

'You dirty bastard,' he said 'c'mon get off my bus.' The young girls giggled at the altercation and finally the young man in front of Jack noticed something was going on and removed his earpieces to find out what. The driver took hold of the man's arm, although weak he allowed himself to be guided swiftly off the bus.

The bus drove away leaving the down and out slouching forlornly on the verge. Jack watched as he collapsed to a seating position in the grass. The bus gathered speed and he soon became a speck in the distance.

Before moving off the driver had begrudgingly sprinkled sick granules over the rough splatter, the stink was now a nauseating mixture of vomit and antiseptic.

Ten minutes later the bus pulled into the station. It was a journey that generally took twice the time, but today the traffic was almost non-existent, they actually arrived on time despite the bus initially being late. A few vehicles went past them in either direction, although the majority were mostly police cars, ambulances or fire engines.

Jack pulled himself up with the aid of the vertical handrail. The passengers kept themselves to themselves as they sauntered off the stationary bus, Jack taking up the rear as his good manners dictated to him to let everyone else go first.

'Bit of a weird day,' he said to the driver as he was counting up his takings.

'Ain't it just,' he replied 'I hope you don't need a ride home mate. We've all been called back to the depot.'

'Really? It must be bad then. Heavy snow didn't stop you guys over winter.' Jack said flabbergasted.

'I know. it's all this talk of this flu bug going round.'

'Tell me about it, I got half my workforce off. And my kids are laid up in bed. Don't think I'll be long at work myself.'

'You take care mate, watch your young ones, radio was saying all sorts of stuff earlier,' the driver said to Jack as he stepped down.

'Yeah, you too,' he replied.

'I'll be alright, it's just me and I'll be locking myself away at home in about an hour. After I've mopped up the mess.'

With a wave back Jack walked away as the doors of the bus slammed closed and the reverse beeper started sounding. Jack walked deep in thought, now concerned for his children, he pushed the thought away, they just have a bit of a fever. He felt uneasy walking through the almost deserted streets towards his offices. Although empty sounds echoed around from all over the area, screams, bumps, bangs and sirens.

As he approached his work place he saw the old tramp that spent most of the day sitting against the building. They never bothered to move him on as he was never any trouble. Rumours always abounded that in reality he lived quite comfortably.

Jack was about to wish him well as he passed but it seemed he was asleep sitting up in his stained baggy duffle coat. He smiled at the irony of sleeping outside while hell was breaking loose.

He jogged up the steps to the glass double doors and bounced off them as he went to push through. They were locked. Puzzled he reached into his bag to retrieve his own set of keys.

The building was still locked up as it had been at close of business the previous night. Even the cleaners hadn't been in by the look of it. He unlocked the door and entered as the continuous drone of the alarm emanated from the control panel around the corner of the foyer. Jack flicked open the cover and punched in the four digit code to unset it.

Before leaving the reception area and heading for his office, he dropped the latch on the front door and checked the switchboard at the receptionist's desk. No messages, very strange considering no-one was in.

His second floor office was as he'd left it a day earlier. He switched on his computer and stared out of the window. The double glazing blocked out all the noise but he could see clearly the strobe effect of the blue lights of emergency vehicles in several different areas of the town.

Taking a seat at his desk he quickly navigated his PC to the news website he regularly used. There was report after report of random acts of violence, general disorder and the sickness that was going round. He clicked on the live feed icon and after a few seconds of buffering the video started to play. All that ran was an emergency message advising people not to travel and stay locked in.

Jack sat back open mouthed. He had the urge to get back to his wife and children as soon as possible. He transferred his wallet and keys from his bag to his pockets and left the office. Jogging down the stairs he thought about how he would get back home.

The foyer was still quiet. He walked across it sorting through his key ring to find the correct one for the main door. He looked up just as a fingerless gloved hand slapped on the glass. Jack jumped back in surprise. The tramp stared back with colourless pupils and iris less eyes, a snarl fixed on his face.

Jack stepped back as the old man thumped more rhythmically on the toughened glass. He headed back beside the reception desks past the rest rooms and kitchen, and headed towards the rear exit. The back door was also locked so he rifled through his keys yet again and unlocked it pushing it open warily. Nothing but the normal mess of a backyard welcomed him.

The yard led to a passageway that exited via the front of the building. He peeked around the corner slowly. The man was still at the front door banging with both hands. Jack stepped out into the open and walked quickly the opposite way.

Until a scream from behind caused him to wheel round. It was Michelle, the receptionist, and it appeared the tramp was attacking her. He ran back to her aid. By the time he reached them Michelle was laying on her back with the tramp on her tearing at her face and neck with his grubby fingers.

With a rush of adrenalin Jack kicked the man in the midriff. It had no effect so he continued kicking him. The man's attention now turned towards him, pink tinged slobber was stringing from his open mouth. He rose up leaving the blood streaked Michelle on the floor sobbing.

He flew at him with surprising speed for an old man. Jack grabbed him by the shoulders and shoved him back as hard as he could. The assailant tripped backwards over the prone figure of the receptionist. As he sprawled onto the steps to the small office block his head connected with the bottom tread with a loud sickening crack. Momentum rolled the body to lie face down on the pavement at right angles to Michele, never to move again.

Michele was close to shock. She cried and shook as Jack helped her into the foyer, ensuring that he locked the door behind them. He made her comfortable on one of the couches in the reception area. He retrieved the company first aid kit from its wall mount in the kitchen.

Kneeling by her he dabbed the wounds with cotton wool and water. She was shivering and had multiple scratches and gouges to her face and neck, thankfully the injuries were much more superficial than the amount of blood suggested.

'Why?' she said with a sob.

Jack gave a nervous laugh 'I wish I knew.'

'He just went for me,' she coughed.

'Well, looking outside and from fragmented news reports it suggests that whatever's occurring has been so fast that no-one knows for sure.'

Michelle suddenly shook with some sort of frenzied fit coursing through her body. Jack sat back not knowing what to do. All of a sudden she arched her back and with a piercing cry she slumped back down onto the couch and was still. He was dismayed and picked up her hand searching her wrist for a pulse but to no avail.

The phones were now all down. Whatever was happening seemed to be escalating into meltdown, and fast. He had been away from home for only a couple of hours. It was obvious no help was forthcoming. He was torn between staying with Michelle's body, as witnesses would be required, and getting home.

It didn't take him too long to decide. Michelle was dead, not knowing what was happening with his family meant there could be a chance they were still alive. He covered Michelle with a clean table cloth he had found in the kitchen and left a note as to what happened and his contact details, although it seemed farcical it's the only thing he had time to do. He left again by the rear exit, but this time he locked it behind him.

Peeking cautiously around the corner for a second time he could see the body of the tramp still lying where it had fallen. The town was starting to look more and more like a warzone. Plumes of smoke were visible along the skyline from various points both close by and further distant. Despite his shock at what was going on he was coming to his senses. Earlier he could only see what was in his face. He was now becoming much more methodical and was planning the tasks needed to get back home to his family.

He moved stealthily along from one doorway and shelter to the next. People passed by, some distraught some looking distinctly sick. He did not want to get involved with either type. His target destination was a car hire company the firm he works for uses. It wasn't far away and they had an account, in fact he was going to use one for the day's chores due to his own being broken down.

The side street was easy to find and sheltered. He was glad to get off the open main drag, it made him feel a bit exposed. The car lot was behind a row of shops, as he approached he could see the gate was already open. The cars closest to the entrance were damaged with broken windows and numerous dents and dings. The glass beads from the shattered windows crunched beneath his feet as he passed by the vehicles carefully.

The door to the small office was smashed. Red slews of what he assumed to be blood were along its sides. He pushed the door into the wrecked office and walked around the counter. The expected dead body was not present, whoever left the blood behind must've been seriously injured. He located the key press, as he'd seen the employees fetch keys from in the past. Its own key was still in the lock.

Jack looked through the grimy window into the lot to pick out an undamaged car and get its registration number. He looked through the keys in the cabinet and located the correct ones quickly. He thought about leaving details as he had done with Michelle's body, but decided not to bother. It didn't look like anyone would come back to the office any time soon.

He drove out of the yard in the compact car and headed in the direction of his home. The majority of the streets were empty and clear, not surprising as it was predominantly a business area with very few people able to afford to live locally. As he passed through the suburbs damage and trouble was far more prevalent. He passed many fraught tired looking members of the emergency services.

At one point he stopped in an effort to explain the situation with Michelle's death. The only reply he received from an exhausted looking police officer was 'Join the club mate'.

The country roads made him more at ease despite having to negotiate a few traffic altercations. His conscience told him he should stop to help, but his heart kept him moving towards his home. He was all the more concerned about his children from what he had seen, he prayed they were not going to end up like some of the people he had seen in town.

As he passed the point where the man was thrown off the bus earlier in the day, he was surprised to see him still there standing now, but very close to the same point. Jack slowed the car and peered at him from the safety of it. He stood motionless with the same vacant eyes as the tramp. As the creature realised the vehicle was near it approached it with outstretched arms and a familiar vicious snarl on its face. Jack had seen enough and accelerated away before he could reach him.

The communal car park was half empty as he pulled the hire car into the space next to his broken down BMW. After locking it he moved briskly across the small communal green area to his house. Using his key he entered and slammed the door behind him.

'Jack?' came the tearful voice of his wife, Ellen, from the kitchen.

'Yes it is, are you okay?' he said as he hurried into the room.

He walked straight over to her and gave her a hug.

'Are you okay?' he said.

'Not really,' she replied her cheeks puffy and moist from crying.

He stepped back noticing that her lower arm was loosely wrapped with a bandage.

'My god, what happened?' he said

'It was David. Both the kids are delirious with the flu. He bit me and Kelly tried too. The TV has been saying all day that it's some sort of apocalypse.'

'What?' he said dismayed.

'I had to shut them in one of the bedrooms, my babies are like animals, and I just don't know what to do,' she said trying hard not to completely crack up and lose control.

'It's okay Ellen,' he said trying to comfort her. 'I'm back now, I'll sort it out.' He said in an effort to put her mind at ease.

Jack left the room and headed upstairs. Before he was halfway up he could hear the thumping on his son's bedroom door. Every parents fear was anything bad happening to their children, Jack knew it wasn't going to be a happy ending. He felt as if he had entered a dream world, nothing felt like he was actually experiencing it, just viewing from afar.

After grabbing a pillow from his and Ellen's room, he held it like a shield and went to the door. He opened and pushed it wide. The children behind it were also pushed back into the room. For a few seconds his son and daughter stared at him through cloudy empty eyes. Tears of realisation ran down Jacks cheeks as they rushed at him. Using the pillow he pushed them hard into the room. He stepped back and slammed the door shut as their small bodies continued to pound onto it. With his back against the door, he slid down to a seated position. He put his head into his hands and cried.

He was unsure how long he had been sitting there but it was dark as he descended the stairs slowly. The electricity was still on, so he turned on the lights as he headed through the house looking for his wife. He soon found her. She was in the lounge laid on the sofa shivering uncontrollably.

He rushed to her side. Sweat dripped from her face and she was running a fever, her forehead felt so hot it would burn his hand.

'I feel really bad,' said Ellen.

'I can see. I'll get you some aspirin or something,' he replied.

'Don't bother, I can't keep them down, I tried,' she said closing her eyes.

Jack held her till she either fell asleep or passed out, he wasn't sure which. He made her comfortable and headed into the kitchen. He took a carton of milk from the fridge and drained it quickly. Hunger was non-existent but he was very thirsty having had no food or drink since breakfast some hours before.

He walked back to the lounge, turned on the TV and collapsed into his usual armchair. He flicked through the channels finding all displayed an official warning test card.

'Stay in your homes. Do not approach other people and remain isolated. If any of your household are suffering from flu-like symptoms, quarantine them in another room for your own safety.'

Jack was living in a nightmare; he had difficulty comprehending what was happening because it was all so fast. Maybe what Ellen said was the truth and it really was the apocalypse or rapture or whatever which religion called it. She now slept on the settee opposite his own chair. Exhaustion was setting in and his eyelids felt heavy. The warning was imprinted on his brain as sleep enveloped him.

He awoke in the early hours, grey light filtered through the closed curtains. The television was still on now showing a new warning. His eyesight steadied and he looked up into the grey face of his wife standing over him. Her eyes were blank and she wore a vicious grimace on her face.

Her lips pealed back showing her teeth as she slowly released a guttural snarl and leapt towards Jack. He threw himself sideways from his chair as Ellen leapt into it. He crouched in disbelief as his confused wife looked around and locked her sights on him yet again. She stood quickly facing him. Jack panicked and punched her in the side of the face almost breaking his hand.

Ellen went down hard and he stepped forward in regret at what he had just done. Something he would never have contemplated. She started scrabbling to her feet unaffected by the heavy blow. He stepped back and paused, then thinking fast he ran through to the kitchen. As he passed the dining set he pulled two of the chairs over onto their backs to hamper her following him. He grabbed the full washing basket on the kitchen side and tipped out the contents rifling through them.

Once she had negotiated the chairs Ellen ran headlong into a bed sheet which Jack wrapped around her. He forced her to the ground and used the sheet to envelope her. Within a quarter of an hour Jack had securely bound her up with an assortment of clothing and bed clothes.

He carried Ellen bound up, back to the settee and sat back in his armchair. He read the new message now displayed on the television screen.

'Emergency Broadcast. After the flu passes the previously infected person is no longer the person you knew. They will try to kill any uninfected person by eating them. To stop them you must cause either severe head trauma or damage to the spinal cord. THIS IS NOT A DRILL.'

Jack sat and contemplated as he stared at the bound body of his wife who still squirmed and stared intently back at him, her vivid blue eyes now a creamy white. In the room above him his children still pummelled at the bedroom door. He knew what must be done. But first he needed to take time to rationalise and find more proof that this was the end. Jack wanted to be perfectly sure he was doing the right thing before committing himself to Hell by murdering his own family.

2 RANDALL

'Have you got my paper Randal?' John shouted from the next level up on the scaffolding. Randal was sitting with his back to the wall, half eaten sandwich in one hand, grubby mug of lukewarm coffee in the other.

'Yeah right, wouldn't wipe my arse on that rag,' he yelled back.

Finishing his mouthful of coffee he placed the mug on the rough planks and turned the page to continue reading the lead story from the cover.

'You Tosser, I can see you reading it through the planks,' came the coarse reply. 'Just pass up the sports page will ya.'

Randal sighed and stood up, after separating the sports section he passed it up to the waiting hand. He retook his seat and glanced at the clock tower a few streets over, from his elevated position three stories up he had a clear and uninterrupted view of it. They still had another twenty minutes of lunch break. He glanced back down to the paper.

Reading the news wasn't something Randal did very often. The headline was just too loud to ignore 'The Dead Rise'. Despite the newspaper being the most unreliable on the market, there was usually a modicum of truth in what was written.

He had seen people falling ill everywhere. For him it was an advantage, some of his work mates had started thinning out giving him a higher chance of more casual jobs on the various sites. With his first child on its way he wanted to straighten up and give his family the best start he could, especially as he'd had such a bad youth himself. His family had never really existed when he was a toddler. He was pushed from pillar to post, and as he grew up he mixed with a crowd where violence was king. He wasn't going to let his offspring follow in his footsteps.

Randal leant back against the wall, tilted his head and closed his eyes dreaming about the future. After only a couple of minutes a shout went up from above him.

'Oi, get away from that gate.'

His eyes snapped open. He looked up to see John above him, leaning against the safety rail. Randal stood and followed John's line of sight directly to the ten foot reinforced wire gate protecting the building site from the busy city street on the other side.

A group of roughly a dozen people were hammering and rocking the fence back and forth. John descended the ladder to Randal's level. He stomped along the boards towards him.

'Back me up mate.' He said as he passed Randal heading for the ladder to the ground.

Randal put down his mug and stuffed the remainder of the sandwich into his mouth and followed. John was in his fifties but was fit and strong for his age, due mainly to a hard life and many years spent working on building sites. The ladder bounced as he hurriedly descended. When he reached the ground Randal followed.

John stood in front of the undulating gate a little taken aback by the condition of the people in front of him. Randal joined him,

'What the hell,' he said as the ragged, pale and obviously sick mob seemed to react angrily to their appearance just a few feet away. John looked around mouth agape. He turned his attention back to the motley group and shouted,

'You lot, get the fuck away from this gate right now.'

They ignored him and continued their manic destruction of the gate. John leaned forward and picked up a discarded offcut of two by four. He banged it on the fence but all it achieved was to get the group more excited and fuel their eagerness to get at them.

'I don't like this,' said Randal 'They ain't right.'

'They're escaped lunatics or something.' John said having to raise his voice over the cacophony. Two more workmen joined them at the entrance just as the top hinges finally gave way. The gates lurched forward making the four men jump back a couple of feet. What looked like a young executive in a suit complete with tie scrambled forward over the rapidly falling fence. Clearing it he got up and lurched straight at John.

'Don't come any closer,' ordered John lifting the makeshift weapon in a defensive position. The man ignored him and lurched forward. John wasn't going to tell him again, and swung the lump of wood connecting it with the assailants head with a loud crack. John hit him with such force that the man flew sideways off his feet.

The fence had finally fallen flat and the rest of the group piled over towards the four men who were now backing away further. They watched as more maniacal people join the group from the street. The man John had laid out was now on his hands and knees and crawling towards Randal. Randal hefted a steel toe-capped boot and kicked the man on his chin. His head flicked back and he flew a full one eighty degrees onto his back, spraying blood and shattered teeth in an arc as he went.

'Nice one,' congratulated John as he swung the improvised club back and forth. All four of the labourers were now locked in battle fending off the attackers. One of them, a plasterer, went down in a hail of thumping, tearing hands. Dry plaster dust flew from his coveralls. He fought back as best he could but sheer numbers overwhelmed him. The dust was replaced by red mist of the man's blood as the ghouls ripped him apart in frenzy.

'Up,' Randal shouted as he backed up towards the ladder. John pushed back the section of the group in front of him gaining valuable seconds which allowed him to run and join Randal at the ladder. He jumped up the first few rungs Randal hot on his tail. The third man followed Randal along with at least fifty of the psychopaths clawing after him. He struggled as many hands grabbed and pulled at his kicking legs. He cried out in frustration and pain. John had already reached the top and hurled bricks and blocks into the crowd below.

Randal had paused halfway up and reached back in an attempt to help his screaming workmate. He grabbed his hand and frantically tried to pull him up. He could see it was in vain as the maniacs were ripping and biting into the man's upper legs and buttocks, the previously white denims he wore were now a deep crimson. Randal released the man's weakening grip and watched him get swallowed up into the ravenous crowd below.

He turned and continued up to join John on the scaffolding. They pulled the ladder up, the building they were working on currently had no internal staircases and the ladder was the only way onto the upper levels. For the moment they were relatively safe.

"It was in your paper,' said Randal steadying his breathing. 'They're zombies.'

'If I hadn't seen it for myself I'd have said you were a nutter.' John replied.

From their elevated position they could see what was happening wasn't just an isolated occurrence. People were running wildly through the streets, all vehicles were at a standstill some crashed into buildings, street furniture and each other. Further out they could see plumes of smoke drifting into the sky at various points. All this was happening to a soundtrack of screams, shouts, crashes and bangs.

'I must get home,' said Randal.

'Don't we all want that, I've got a sawn off shotgun at home that's been waiting for something like this,' he replied with a crooked grin.

'Seriously mate, Steph will need me. The kids due in less than a month, she's a tough bird but not enough to cope with this shit,' his concern showed.

'Wanna make a run for it?' John said rooting around the tool boxes on the platform. He turned and handed a claw hammer and hatchet towards Randal,

'Which one?'

'Both,' Randal replied taking them from him. He emptied has tool belt of loose nails and slid the hammer into a loop on it. John turned around brandishing a sledge hammer.

'It's been a while since I killed someone. This time I might even get away with it,' John said smiling.

'I always thought you were a closet psycho.' Randal replied.

'Oh no mate I'm far more methodical than that. I spent the eighties robbing post offices and scrapping at football matches. And I loved it.'

The large group of ghouls were gathered under the scaffolding craning their necks and reaching up to the two men twenty feet above them. Randal looked over the edge.

'I make it fifty five give or take a couple,' he said aloud when he had finished mentally counting.

'There's no more coming in the gate, so if we can finish a good few of them from up here we might be in with a chance of getting away.'

John turned towards the building and grabbed a couple of bricks from one of the stacks dotted along the scaffolding. He leaned over the edge and taking careful aim launched it at one of the upturned faces below.

The projectile smashed into the woman's face so hard she instantly collapsed into a heap and didn't get up. Randal followed Johns lead and started throwing bricks into the group.

Within ten minutes the horde was reduced to less than a dozen.

'Okay. Let's go,' John said.

They grabbed the ladder and ran with it to the opposite end of the platform. Together they dropped the it down to the ground, as it hit John threw the sledgehammer down and descended. By the time he had reached the base Randal was already halfway down. John retrieved his weapon just as Randal joined him.

The remainder of the group were awkwardly heading towards them. The men had space and speed on their side. They headed to the gate passing through the ever decreasing gap between them and the insane people. Their boots rattled over the downed gate as they hurried out into what looked like a warzone.

It was hard to tell survivors from aggressors, they avoided all people which wasn't hard as they were few and far between. They walked briskly, constantly looking around trying to spot danger before it happened.

The predominant colour was red. There were splatters of it everywhere, as well as bodies and limbs. It was as if a combine harvester had driven down the street.

John stopped Randal.

'This is where we part mate.'

'Are you sure? It's easier to watch each other's back,' said Randal.

'You got your woman to get back to, I'm just gonna head to the West End. With all this chaos I'm gonna get some payback, have a party, kick some ass and probably go out with a bang.' The crooked grin returned.

They shook hands.

'Good luck mate'

John jogged over to a relatively new Jaguar abandoned in the middle of the road. He noted the keys still hanging from the ignition.

'Hell I might as well go in style,' he shouted back to Randal. He sat in the seat and started the engine pulling the door shut. He glanced back to see Randal had already disappeared. He revved the engine and shot off with a squeal of the tyres.

As Randal reached the block of flats he could see his fears were not unfounded. The security door at the main entrance was ajar, its lock casing hanging limp on a splintered frame. He quietly picked his way through discarded items and blood trails all along the ground floor corridor. He edged past open doors to apartments tentatively. He reached the stairwell to the second floor which resembled the ground floor. He headed up the last flight which was where the flat he shared with his girlfriend was situated.

His floor had fared no better than the previous ones. There was a figure further along the corridor. He tiptoed closer not really wanting to see as he feared the worst. The hunched figure of a man had his back to him and was crouching over what looked like the remains of an animal. As he neared the macabre mess he realised an animal carcass wouldn't wear nail polish. A sob slipped from his lips, the man's head spun round in an instant, face covered in blood with entrails hanging in the sides of its mouth. Randal rushed at the man in fury, he attacked with such speed that the ghoul had barely risen to a crouch. He buried the hatchet to its hilt in the man's forehead. The monster was slain with the axe stuck; Randal pulled the already gory hammer from his belt and proceeded to smash the things head into flat pulp.

He stood silently gazing out of the window at the dying city. Fear was a very rare feeling for Randal. He could not turn and face the body of his girlfriend. As a few minutes turned to an hour the fear shifted and he did turn around. He could barely recognise the lump of savaged dead meat lying by the wall as his Steph but it was her. Next to her lay a perfectly formed but dead child, whose umbilical cord was still attached within the gaping void which used to be his girlfriend's torso. There was a peaceful look to his baby sons' face.

The fear was now gone, he seethed with pure hatred.

3 SIMON

'Come on mate, I gotta make money too. Twenty quid each is just way too much,' said the skinhead.

'Get lost these things retail at a ton fifty each, you want them at twenty five each otherwise you wouldn't still be standing here Gary,' said Simon feigning closing the trunk on the booty.

'You fucker, you got me pegged,' he spat in the palm of his hand and offered it to Simon 'done two fifty for the lot.'

Simon fished in his pocket and passed a bottle of hand cleanser to Gary 'Wipe your hands before you shake mine, this ain't the nineteen forties you know, haven't you heard something's going around.'

Money exchanged hands and Gary motioned to a couple of youths standing nearby loitering near a corner. Simon started passing out the boxes sporting the latest games console on their packaging.

'That reminds me, I'm getting asked about weapons. Can you get any guns?' said Gary

'No mate, that's out of my league,' Simon lied. With his connections he could get pretty much anything, but not for a two bit pimp cum drug dealer like Gary. He was just too insane and would probably end up dropping him in it, which was never going to happen.

'Have you tried Stax?' he suggested.

'Ain't you heard? He's a goner.'

Simon paused with a couple of boxes in his hands genuinely surprised.

'What? I saw him yesterday!'

'Happened last night, it was a fucking bloodbath by all reports.' Gary continued 'They reckon some of his whores got fed up with the beatings and ripped him apart. Literally.'

Simon had heard more and more reports like that, along with the crap about zombies walking the streets he always took what people like Gary said with a pinch of salt, but nowadays there was bound to be some truth in there somewhere. After concluding his business with Gary he shut the trunk on his XJ6 and got back behind the wheel. He fished in his pocket and chucked the last few packets of his tablets marked up as De-animate into the glove compartment.

He was glad to get rid of the game consoles. They were pretty damn hot having only been liberated from an electronics store by some little scrote the previous night. Ironically the aforementioned thief probably scored his drugs from Gary, which means it was likely that Simon had just taken back some of the cash that he'd paid the lad for the consoles in the first place. He smiled as he counted the notes into his own substantial wad of cash, which he returned back to his inside pocket.

He drove carefully along the small alleyway with a grumble of the powerful motor. At the junction the traffic he needed to join was at a standstill. He thumped the steering wheel with impatience.

'What the hell are they protesting about this time?' he uttered. Whenever the traffic was this solid it was usually whining students complaining they're skint or some minority saying it just ain't fair. A thump brought him back to reality as a scruffy woman ran into the front wing of his car. He opened the door and jumped out.

'What the fuck, watch where you're going!' he shouted.

She looked up through strands of matted long hair, dried blood was prevalent around her face and down the front of her once white blouse. Her mouth was pulled into a scowl and as her misty eyes met Simons she launched herself onto the bonnet and scrabbled on the polished paintwork to get at him.

Simon knew the difference between a manic threat and just plain angry, so he jumped back into the car as the assailant pulled herself over the bonnet gripping the strut of the windscreen to get across. He slammed the door shut almost severing the fingers from the girl's hand. She seemed to ignore the pain from an injury that would debilitate a normal person. She banged and scraped at the window with her free hand, as if trying to gain entry to get to him. This just wasn't the common flu bug. There was something very, very wrong with this girl. Simon was a tough guy, but the action of this thing scared the crap out of him.

He released the door slightly allowing the girls hand to be removed, and then quickly slammed it shut again. Now she was free she thumped on the side window with renewed vigour. Then someone ran around the corner almost colliding with his bonnet where the first girl had. But this person was uninfected; the fear was evident on his face. The infected woman instantly turned her attention from the unobtainable Simon to the new arrival out in the open and within her reach.

She leapt back onto the bonnet grabbing hold of the stunned teenage boy on the opposite side. Simon watched in frozen terror as the infected girl ripped and tore at the youths flailing form. She dug her teeth into his wide open mouth and tore his top lip off spraying blood across the cars wing. The screams from the boy were shrill and piercing. The girl ripped and tore at him ferociously.

Simon still sat behind the wheel thirty minutes after the screaming had stopped and the girl had gone off to chase down another screaming pedestrian. She left the broken corpse of the youth lying on the crimson coated bonnet.

The traffic on the main road in front of him was going no-where. All the cars, vans and trucks were abandoned by their drivers. Simon leant across to the glove compartment on the passenger side and dropped down its door exposing an array of receipts and parking tickets. He haphazardly shovelled them out into the foot well and onto the passenger seat with shaking hands until the small cloth wrapped item at the bottom was accessible. He unwound the rag from around his snub nosed .38 revolver and checked to ensure the six shells were still in situ in the cylinder.

Simon flipped open his mobile phone and rifled through the contacts. He stopped on 'Mum', selected the number and put the phone up to his ear. All that could be heard was the continuous tone of no such number. He swore and looked down at the LCD screen 'No Service'. He desperately needed to know that his mother was okay. The nursing home she was resident at was no more than a couple of miles away.

The dull screams and cries of the city became much clearer as he opened the door and tentatively got out. He suspected he'd never see his beloved old Jag again but he locked it anyway, just in case the crisis had blown over in a week or so.

He held the pistol down by his side as he cautiously stepped out of the alley and onto the log jammed street. Very few people were around but those who were seemed to be runny with purpose. The pavement was a mess of discarded shopping, briefcases, backpacks and glass shards from the numerous shop windows along the road. He headed towards the nursing home in a quick walk, continually looking around for any threats.

Whilst looking round he ploughed straight into a man coming quickly out of a shop. Simon kept his feet but the other person splayed out onto the pavement.

'Oh shit! I'm so sorry,' he said as he offered the man a hand to get up. What looked like a smartly dressed businessman looked up at him. His fringe parted to show a snarl and similar empty eyes to the girl from earlier. Simon jumped back and instinctively raised the pistol.

To his astonishment the obviously infected man scrambled awkwardly to get up on his feet.

'Get back mate, I'm warning you,' Simon said as he stepped back. The beast growled as he stumbled towards him.

'I'm gonna shoot, get back.'

The man ignored what he said and continued towards him. Simon pulled the trigger. The loud pop shocked him as the bullet left the short barrel and hit the man square in the chest. It made the infected man miss a step and after a short pause he continued coming at him. Simon fired twice more as the he backed up and the man fell to the floor but instantly tried to get to his feet again. Simon didn't hang around this time. He sidestepped past him and hurried away. He kept looking back and saw the guy get back to his feet. Now Simon was further away he seemed to just saunter off in the opposite direction. If Simon didn't know better he'd say the guy was a zombie like the press had been saying. He considered that maybe this time the press hadn't been overreacting after all.

He travelled as fast as he could through the urban warzone that had been the affluent high street of this city suburb. He gave a wide berth to anyone he came across, infected or not. His one task was to get to his mother, his only living relative, and make sure she was okay. On a good day she was lucid, on a bad day she didn't know who he was at all. The unpredictability of age and dementia was frustrating.

The nursing home was in a quiet tree lined avenue. It had an impressive Edwardian frontage and was set back from the road. Simon spent more money on his mother's comfort than his own, although he wasn't starving by any stretch of the imagination. He walked up the path towards the front door. He noticed there were no cars in the adjacent car park.

Next to the large black front door was a number pad. Simon quickly tapped in his code and pushed the door open. The reception area was normally spotless, but not today. Paperwork was strewn around and a computer screen lay shattered on the floor. He edged into the corridor that led past the ground floor rooms and headed to the staircase up to the first floor.

There was an ever present odour in the air of urine and faeces, along with the sound of calls for help and crying. Simon had already got an idea of what had happened; the entire staff had just bugged out leaving all the residents to wallow in their own filth.

He entered the stairwell and jogged up to the next level. The sounds and smells were much the same as the ground floor but not so much debris. He headed for his mother's room. He knocked on the door and tried the handle, it was unlocked. He peeked around the door to see his mother sitting in her wheel chair looking out of the window at the ornamental garden below. He sighed with relief that she hadn't become infected, the last thing he wanted was for his dear old mum to suffer.

She turned her wheelchair and squinted towards him.

'Is that my Joshua?' Said the elderly woman as Simon entered.

'No mum, its Simon.'

'Well you look like my husband. He said he'd be back today.'

'Come on mum, dads been dead for fifteen years'

'Oh, you must be Simon then, my little baby boy,' she smiled.

'Yes mum, it's me.' He returned the smile.

'I've been ringing the buzzer all morning but no-one comes,' she said concerned.

'I know, I'm here now.'

'I have a bit of a problem Simon. I've made a bit of a mess. Go and get your dad to help me.'

'Okay mum, I'll get him.' She turned her wheelchair back towards the window as Simon turned towards the door. He paused for a moment and looked at his mother's back.

'I love you mum,' he said as he raised the revolver, his eyes watering slightly.

'I love you too, Joshua.'

4 MEETING

The grotesque figure gorged itself on the innards of a fallen woman. Her body was twisted and broken. Her open mouth and wide eyes were fixed into a thousand yard stare caused by her sudden death. Her naked flesh was splattered with the almost black blood, the type that comes from deep within. The hands of the fowl smelling assailant delved and tugged at internal organs from the ripped open stomach and chest cavity. It chewed on them with a voracious appetite, one born from instinct rather than hunger. The dead no longer has an appetite or any other senses for that matter. All they knew was hunger, an intense instinctive starvation only satiated by warm meat. They were merely automatons, like a wind-up toy that never seemed to wind down.

What the corpse didn't know was that the hard steel object that shattered its skull mere milliseconds later was that of a police issue extendable baton.

'The rotten stinking piece of crap, she looked like she was hot as well,' said Simon.

'Yeah and in about ten minutes she'll bite your cock off,' smiled Randal as he plunged the stiletto dagger into the forehead of the freshly butchered victim.

The men were tough. They had been long before the dead started rising and the world fell apart, but in different ways. Both had difficult childhoods.

Simon's childhood was secure and loving; until his father lost his job and they ended up living on next to nothing on a run-down housing estate. To make matters worse he became the sole breadwinner after his father had committed suicide. Simon was smart and used his good looks and witty banter to get his way.

Randal grew up on a similar estate, the difference being that his mother was an alcoholic, and his father could have been any number of men. He fended for himself for most of his young life, and lived from house to house with relatives. Once the school had taught him to read and write he left, never to return until he burgled the computer lab. He too was intelligent, but lacked etiquette and was scarred from many past battles before the world went bad.

They looked out from the rooftop of the six story office block. Below in the street the horde was growing ever larger.

'Oops, that went a bit wrong,' said Simon with a nervous grin.

'You think? The idea was to lose them not get them to advertise our whereabouts to every infected in the city,' said Randal as he playfully clouted Simon round the head.

Looking over the crowd of infected below with a pair of binoculars Simon noticed some faster movement on the edge of his vision.

'Shit, there's someone down there.'

Randal followed Simons gaze past the group gathered below. He saw the figure in the distance. It was obvious it wasn't an Isaiah as it walked quickly and more importantly with purpose. Something the Isaiah effect victims don't have.

'Let me see,' said Randal making a grab for the binoculars. Simon gave them up still looking down to the new arrival. Randal focused them on the figure that was now closing in on the group below.

'What the hell is he doing? He's heading straight into them.'

Randal could now make out more detail. He was a tall slim man who looked reasonably athletic. He wore jeans and a long sleeve button up shirt. He appeared to be carrying nothing but a baseball bat in one hand and something that resembled a rock climber's pick hanging from his other fist.

At estimation he would say the guy was just a little older than himself and Simon. He lowered the binoculars as the outer members of the group had noticed the newcomer. The man ploughed in using the bat to push them away and the pick to batter them.

'He's gone psycho,' said Simon wide eyed.

'Naw mate, he just hates em.' Randal replied as he turned to quickly leave the roof top. Simon grabbed his jacket and swung it on as he followed.

It took them a good five minutes to make it to the ground floor. The expansive foyer was a mess of torn paper but clear of large obstacles. Reinforced gates covered the Plexiglas frontage. They could see that the infected group was distracted by the newcomer and that worked to their advantage.

They moved quickly through to the back door. As they cut through the dustbin area with its piles of liquefied rubbish causing a slippery sheen to the small pathway they had previously created.

The two men continually covered each other as they rounded corners and negotiated obstacles. Randal carried a pump action shotgun and Simon his machete. They moved out into the alleyway that led to the street out front, they could see a few infected milling around.

They stealthily crept up to the entrance and peered around to see the majority of the horde surrounding an ornamental lamp post. Hanging from it was the man they had seen from above. Clinging to it with one arm still tightly hanging onto the pick the other, he was holding the bat flailing wildly at the hands and heads of his attackers.

'Around and in,' whispered Randal pointing out a sparse area to the back of the monument.

They ran out heading around the outside of the pack, Simon slashed at any of the infected that got too close.

Randal could see the man was beginning to tire. He stopped, pumped a shell into the barrel and took careful aim just away from the survivor into the crowd close to him. A boom echoed around the tall buildings, followed by three more pumps and shots in short succession.

The momentary clearance around the man was all the time they needed for rushing in and grabbing him. Simon ducked as the bat missed his head by a whisker.

'Hold on mate, we're rescuing you,' he shouted.

The man allowed Simon to drag him towards Randal who was covering them both with the shotgun. Simon reached Randal who dropped the gun down to one hand and grabbed the new arrivals free arm.

'We're gonna drag ya mate, just go with it,' he said.

'Okay' the man replied exhaustedly.

They ran back towards the alleyway, the man half ran and was half dragged as the two rescuers took his weight. They stumbled through the wedged open door. Simon and the other survivor collapsed in a heap on the other side. Randal turned as an infected approached him. He pumped the gun and raised it to view down the sightline. He then waited.

When the Isaiah was no more than two feet away from him, he pulled the trigger. The body dropped like a stone as the contents of its skull splattered on the walls on either side of the alley. He kicked the fire door shut its lock banged into place. Randal turned and threw the shotgun aside.

'That was the last of the shotgun shells.' He smiled and helped both the men to their feet. He looked into the face of the newcomer.

'Hungry?' he said.

'God yes,' he said with a smile.

They took the stairs up to the roof. Randal led the way explaining how they had been living on the roof of the block for the past couple of weeks. He also filled the man in on how he and Simon had met: they had both decided to scavenge weapons from a police station at the same time.

Randal reached the last door and pushed it open.

'Welcome to our domain,' Simon said.

The man walked around in awe of what the guys had achieved. It was like walking around in a campsite complete with tents, Astroturf, a washing line and a massive barbecue.

'Wow, you guys have done a great job here, I've never really thought about having a base. I've just been bopping my way through the ghouls. I was hoping to take out as many as I can before they got me. I thought I was the only one left.'

He turned towards his two saviours.

'I owe you my life, thank you.' He held out his hand. Randal was the first to extend his, and they shook hands firmly.

'My name's Jack.'

5 SARAH

Charlotte and Sally sat at the kitchen table eating their breakfast whilst Sarah leant at the opposite counter sipping at her hot black coffee.

'It makes a change them being so quiet first thing.' Dan, Sarah's husband said as he stood at the doorway smiling.

'Where are you off to anyway?' said Sarah walking over to him.

'I got a message, all time off is cancelled. I have to report in, the shits hitting the fan in the city.' he replied quietly so only Sarah could hear.

She pulled him into the hallway out of earshot of the kids.

'But Dan, you only got off shift last night, they can't do that. You're exhausted,' she implored.

'I have no choice. They're short of officers due to this flu outbreak, especially firearms trained ones.' He continued 'It's looking bad all over; I've left the key in my gun safe, the Beretta you've used before is in there. I can't be too specific but if anyone, I mean anyone, even if you know them tries to attack you. Don't hesitate to use it.'

Sarah was shocked.

'Is it really that bad?'

'Look, in town it is. But out here we're fine. Just be on guard, that's all I'm saying,' he smiled.

Dan turned, walked into the kitchen and greeted his daughters.

'Hello my girlies.'

'Daddy, daddy,' said Charlotte with glee. 'Are you going to take us to school today?'

'I'm afraid not I've got to go to work,' he said as he left her to make himself a coffee.

'Aw,' Charlotte said as she finished her breakfast.

Sarah lingered in the hallway then she snapped out of her thoughts and re-entered the kitchen.

'Come on girls get your shoes on,' she said then stood beside her husband and touched his hand. He turned to her and both smiling they embraced.

'We all love you here so please make sure you come back.'

'Of course I will.'

'Yuck, they're doing it again,' said Sally in disgust at their parent's behaviour.

Sarah grabbed her hand bag and keys. Two minutes earlier she had received a phone call from her girls' school. They had a problem involving some of the students, thankfully her children were not harmed, but they were going to close the school for the time being and she had to collect them immediately.

She held her hand up to the door handle and thought for a moment. She contemplated getting the pistol remembering her husband's words earlier, but then decided against it. She walked to her mini parked in the driveway. The road outside was unusually quiet for a weekday lunchtime.

The drive to the school was uneventful but once she got there it looked as if all hell had broken loose. Parents were crowded at the gate collecting their children; once they had them they rushed them away to the waiting cars. Two police vehicles and an ambulance were parked haphazardly in the playground, blue lights still revolving.

She hastily parked the car in a space recently vacated as she drove up, the stern driver keen on getting away from the school. She was already walking away from the car as the door slammed. People were briskly walking away from the gates dragging crying children, heads down, intent on getting away as fast as possible.

'Laura,' she called out to another of the mums as she reached the bustling gate. 'What's going on?'

'Haven't you heard? The head and deputy head have both been murdered.'

Panic set in and she desperately clawed her way through to the cordoned off entrance just as two tearful youngsters passed under the tape as they headed for their waiting mother. Two harassed looking police officers were busy keeping the group under control. Sarah recognised one of them.

'Mike, Mike,' she called

He looked towards her and raised his eyebrows in recognition. He moved along the tape to her.

'Hello Sarah.'

'What's the situation? I'm here to get my girls, ones in Cedar class and the other is in pre-school. My friend says Mr Dennison was murdered, is that true?'

Mike looked round and then motioned Sarah towards a less busy area of the cordon.

'It's true. Mr Dennison and Miss Shoebridge are dead. Let me assure you none of the kids have been harmed,' he confided.

'What happened?' she said feeling somewhat calmer knowing all the children were fine.

'I'm not supposed to say anything but considering you're in the job.' He lowered his voice so no-one could overhear. 'It appears Miss Shoebridge walked into the hall to find Jim Seddon, the janitor, using Mr Dennison's head as a mop. The whole floor is smeared with streaks of blood. Miss Shoebridge pretty much froze on the spot and Seddon proceeded to rip her apart. Thanks to the quick thinking secretary he didn't get out of the hall. On hearing the commotion she took one look inside then slammed and chained the doors. She rang us immediately then contacted all the parents to collect their children.'

'Oh, my god!' she said stunned.

'Wait here, I'll get the girls. They're in Cedar and pre-school you say?'

'Um, yes they are,' said Sarah thoughtfully.

She couldn't believe what she had just heard. Jim Seddon was a cheery man, very happy and always eager to help out. He had even changed a punctured tyre she received outside the school one afternoon. She could see Mike heading back towards her hand in hand with Charlotte and Sally. She felt relief as Mike lifted the police tape and lead the girls through to their mother.

'There you go, Sarge, all safe and sound,' he said as she knelt to give them a hug.

'The job was a long time ago Mike, it's just Sarah now,' she smiled. 'Thanks for your help, take care of yourself.'

'Just one thing Sarah,' he said as he leant forward and lowered his voice again 'Go straight home, lock yourself in tight. This sort of thing is happening all over town, and now it appears to be spreading outwards.'

She drove home cautiously with Mike's words on her thoughts. The mood in the streets seemed to have deteriorated to urgency. People and vehicles all seemed to have places to get. The majority of the shops along her way appeared to be either shut or in the process of closing.

Just a couple of streets away from home as Sarah was approaching a junction a green saloon car slewed around the corner broadsiding towards her. Sarah performed an emergency stop in time to see the car correct itself and continue on its way at a fast rate of knots.

Still stationary she dropped her head breathing deeply with relief. A thump on the passenger side of the windscreen jolted her upright, the girls were sobbing in the back. It was a down and out windscreen cleaner, the type that tried to do something other than beg for their money. They often hung out at that particular junction. They would forcibly clean windscreens for a donation to their alcohol fund. There was something not quite right about this guy. His bucket swung empty, rattling against the bodywork of the mini. He was slapping his free hand on her windscreen while he stared directly at her with a frozen grimace and empty white eyes.

She sprang into action immediately accelerating round the junction, glancing at his shrinking figure in the mirror she saw him pirouette then continue stumbling on. She eased down the power, driving more carefully eager to get home safely.

'Don't worry girls we're nearly home,' she said to comfort them.

Their road was virtually deserted with the only thing out of the ordinary being the lack of anyone around. She pulled up on her drive and killed the engine. She looked around to check it was safe then got out of the car, still being observant she tilted the front seat forward to allow the girls to exit. They skipped up to the front door. After entering Sarah made sure the house was safe. Nothing untoward was present so she checked that the doors and windows were secure and she took the girls upstairs.

They spent the next few hours playing together in their room with their mother joining in. By seven o'clock Sarah tucked Charlotte, Sally and her ever present cuddly toy, Pyewacket, into their matching pink princess beds. After getting only half way through their bedtime story both the girls were asleep. She wasn't surprised as it had been a tiring day for all of them.

She sat on the sofa downstairs and thought hard about what both Mike and her husband Dan had said to her. It seemed quite obvious that the authorities knew a lot more about what was going on than the population in general.

As the sun went down and the minutes clicked by Sarah became more and more concerned about Dan. Twelve hours was a long shift, but usually the maximum when she worked the beat. He had been gone for fourteen now. She flicked on the television to be greeted by channel after channel of static and white noise. She turned it off and tossed the remote onto a cushion as she headed for the sound system. The radio also hissed back with nothing but static. She switched that off as well and sat back down on the sofa continuing with her thoughts.

Sarah woke up suddenly. Something had roused her from her sleep on the couch. A loud noise awoke her but she was in the mid stage of sleep unable to pinpoint the noise as real or a dream. Darkness surrounded her. She heard a metallic creak from outside which pushed her into action. The heavy curtains were drawn around the bay window. She pulled them open a crack and peered out.

The night was dark as the streetlight across the road from their driveway was out. It looked like most were but the horizon was lit up by orange glows of varied intensity. There was a van embedded in the wall at the entrance to their drive way. The engine appeared to have died on impact as the only light was the interior one. It was a police van.

'Dan!' She exhaled.

She moved as quickly as possible through to the hall way and headed for the cupboard under the stairs. She opened it and felt around on the wall and grabbed the powerful torch from its charging cradle.

'Mummy, mummy, what was that noise?' Charlotte called from upstairs.

'It's okay sweetheart, go back to bed,' she replied.

Sarah swiftly but tentatively opened the front door. The sounds and odours of a night of disarray assaulted her senses. There was a pervading smell of burning in the air and distant sounds of general disorder with occasional bangs, bumps and screams.

She thought for a moment of getting the gun from the safe. The only thing out of the ordinary in the vicinity was the crashed police van.

She pulled the front door to, leaving it on the latch, and jogged over to the wreck. The door was ajar and a figure in police uniform was slumped over the steering wheel. Before pulling the injured man back instinct kicked in and she checked around his head, neck and shoulders for any serious breakages. With none obviously present she pulled him carefully back to a seated position.

'Mike?'

He coughed and spluttered spraying a mixture of saliva and blood down his chin.

'Sarge, thank god,' he wheezed.

'I have a first aid kit in the house.' She replied while she hastily checked over the rest of him. His legs were crushed and twisted within the metal of what used to be the foot well.

'No time Sarge,' he said between rapid breaths, 'Dan's in the back.' Mike's eyelids fluttered and he grimaced as another wave of pain wracked through his body.

Sarah managed to locate the keys in the steering column. As she grabbed them Mike gripped her arm.

'He's hurt Sarah, really bad.'

She swallowed hard and pulled away from him rushing to the rear of the vehicle. The key slid into the lock effortlessly and she pulled at the handle swinging the door wide. She aimed the light inside to see the prone figure of her husband lying on the floor.

'Oh my god, Dan!' She said bringing her hand up to her mouth in shock. Acting fast she did as she had done with Mike and checked him over for any serious injury. He had many lacerations and was drenched in blood but there were no obvious signs of breakages. He was unconscious which would make moving him a dead weight.

Sarah grabbed the shoulder straps of his body armour and dragged him out of the van and positioned him into a seated position on the tailgate. She threw his arm around her neck and with hidden strength she lifted him into a fireman's lift. She lurched with the extra weight as she carried him up the drive. She pushed through the front door and roughly laid the unconscious Dan down on the hallway floor.

She turned and headed back out to the wreck. Mike was still in position breathing heavily. She grabbed the open driver's door and yanked it in a rocking motion. After six or seven movements the hinges gave which allowed the door to be turned back on itself giving Sarah more room to work on Mikes trapped legs.

'Just leave me Sarge, I'm wedged in tight. I've been bitten by some psycho too. I'm totally screwed,' he wheezed.

Sarah looked around in frustration. Two people were stumbling along the opposite side of the road,

'Hey, over here, I need some help,' she shouted over to them.

'No Sarah, you can't trust anyone,' Mike coughed.

'But I can't get you out of here on my own,' she said frustrated.

The figures altered course and were now heading towards them.

'Go Sarge, get in the house and lock yourself in right now,' he said quickly as he produced a service revolver, clutching it to his chest.

'But they can help.'

Mike gritted his teeth 'Everyone out there is infected with something. We've lost control of the streets. I was at the station with about fifty other officers including Dan. We were the only ones that got out. Those fuckers were eating my friends, EATING them.'

Sarah nervously looked back at the approaching people. Their silhouettes were tripping and stumbling towards them in a stiff uncoordinated gait. She looked back at Mike,

'Thank you,' she said and ran back to the house slamming the door behind her.

Mike tried to position himself in such a way that he could see the approaching threat. It was difficult as he could not feel anything from his chest down. Suddenly the first one was at his side. It was a youth not more than twenty years old. His eyes were cloudy white and he sported bloodless gouges along the side of his face. He reached out to attempt grabbing hold of Mike with a snarl. He fired the pistol into its chest which jolted the youth back a couple of feet. This action made room for the second aggressor to slip in and tear at the raw meat of his legs. Mike placed the barrel of the pistol against the matted hair on the head of the second youth and fired. The front of the van was filled with a cloud of cordite as the first assailant resumed his attack. Mike pushed the gnashing teeth away from his face and with his other hand raised the gun to his own temple and pulled the trigger.

Sarah slammed the door and fell back against it as the first of three shots rang out from behind. She dropped to her knees and scrabbled along the floor in the dull light of dawn. Dan was gone. Screaming from upstairs forced her into action. She followed the sounds of commotion into the girl's room. Muffled crying could be heard coming from her daughters' wardrobe as Dan pawed and moaned at the closed doors.

'Dan, please no!' Sarah sobbed. He immediately stopped and stared back at her in the doorway. He outstretched his hands and started towards her. She backed onto the landing leading him away from her girls. She walked quickly into the bedroom they shared, she threw the curtains open to allow more of the dull daylight in and opened the built in closet. Dan had entered the room as she fumbled with the key to the gun safe bolted to the back wall on the floor.

She kicked out as clammy cold hands tried to grab her. The lock clicked and she pulled the small heavy door open as she turned on her back to kick out at what used to be her husband. She pulled out the gun pouch and tore at it to remove the berretta. She turned round to face Dan who bore over her in a crouch. Sarah thumbed off the safety and with tearful eyes pulled the trigger. Click. Dan came in to continue his assault. On her back she curled up into a foetal position and with all her might kicked out. Both feet connected with Dan's chest catapulting him over to the opposite side of the room. She had bought valuable seconds and turned to root around in the safe for the clip. She found it, turned and rammed it into the grip of the pistol. Dan was back on his feet and was coming at her a vicious grimace on his face. She aimed at his face and pulled the trigger. He dropped like a stone as brain tissue, blood and bone sprayed the wall by the bed.

Sarah let the pistol drop through her fingers and onto the floor. She cradled herself and the tears flowed.

6 FRED

Fred and the sun had been up for five hours before he walked along the path to the local newsagent. He trudged along in his well-worn wellington boots. He'd already fed and milked the small amount of animals he kept, after breakfast he would take the tractor up to the top field and make a start on preparing the ground for onions.

He was regular as clockwork. At nine sharp he cut across the fields and headed into the village to pick up his paper. Then back to the house for a mug of tea and some bacon and eggs before returning to work at ten.

Farming had never been his first choice as a career. It was a family farm and he inherited it from his mother and father who passed away much too soon for him. They both died in a car accident when he was just fifteen. He was all set to go on to Art College and hopefully a career in some sort of design.

Once the paperwork was signed and the farm was his, he never drew a single picture again. He spent many nights of the early years in the lonely farmhouse crying, both for the loss of his family and that of his future ticked by.

As the years clocked up he settled down to life in the country, not that it was too hard as he had always lived there and had helped his father with the chores from the moment he started walking. After some time letting the farm run into disrepair he finally gave in and knuckled down. He worked hard and finally reaped the benefits by having produce that was very popular for quality and price in the local area.

He too was a well-respected member of the community. He was eager to help at the village fetes and events supplying hay bales, machinery and animals for the children to pet. He was charming but only if people could get past his appearance. His bushy grey beard and unkempt hair often made strangers uneasy, thinking he was some sort of tramp in his great coat and dusty corduroys. But to those who knew him he was farmer Fred, charming to the ladies and courteous to the men, and even had the occasional sweet in his pocket for the children, but nit someone to get on the wrong side of.

Despite his popularity he never married. In his youth he chased many a local girl. But more and more he found himself preferring his own company. And now in his mid-fifties what urges he had he dealt with in his own way.

'Good Morning Fred." Delores said from behind the counter as he entered the shop. The bell above the door still echoed his arrival. She was in her early thirties with a mass of blonde hair in a ponytail that almost reached down to the top of her flowery summer skirt. Fred liked her and often fanaticised about her. Not that he ever would proposition her outright. When it came down to it he was still shy. He settled for cheeky banter instead.

'Beautiful day Dolores,' he replied with a smile as he picked up and folded a newspaper from the pile. He fished around in his pocket for some change.

'It's a sorry state with all these riots goin' on in the city,' she said in a gruff voice.

'Yes, very sad. They'll know about it if they come anywhere near my place,' he said with a smile. 'I'll introduce them to my double barrelled friend Purdy.'

'You're a bad man,' she said with a cheeky smile.

'You don't know the half of it, if you were ten years older,' he said with a wink.

'Oooo a cheeky one at that, be off with yer Fred.' She said as she sneezed, then immediately slipped a handkerchief from her sleeve and wiped her red nose.

'Excuse me,' she said nasally

'Sounds like you got a cold coming, I'd go back to bed if I were you, I could tuck you in,' he said raising his eyebrows.

'I'll take some aspirin and carry on, now away with yer, you mucky bugger.' The edges of her smile showing either side of the hanky.

He handed over the change and bade Delores a farewell. He stood outside and let the door close behind him the bell ringing his departure. After breathing in a lung full of clear morning air he headed back towards his home.

As he strolled along the track he flicked the pages of the tabloid. The front page headline shouted out 'Total disorder caused by Isaiah.' He had noticed in recent days the biblical name being tossed around in the press and on the television.

'Bloody scaremongers.' He said aloud as he folded up the rag and continued on his way home.

Half an hour later he was placing his cleaned up mug on the draining board by the sink. Fred wasn't the tidiest of people but he did clean up after meals. Ensuring he never ate from a dirty plate. He was convinced most infection came from sloppy housekeeping in the kitchen.

He closed the back door behind him and headed to the barn across the yard. It was of the open variety and acted as a shelter for his pride and joy. He had saved hard for his four wheel drive Ford Powerstar. The previous tractor, with no cab and just two wheel drive, stood rusting away beside the barn was now made obsolete the more powerful newcomer.

The engine turned over and started with ease, leaving it to warm up Fred stepped down and sauntered over to the harrow attachment in the row of machinery. After preparing it he went back to the chugging hulk and manoeuvred it into position to attach the tool set.

Before retaking his seat he fished about beneath it.

'Let's have some Mahler today.' He said as he slammed the cassette into the deck mounted just above his eye line. As the orchestral movement started and the choristers began their singing, Fred drove from the yard and headed up the track that would take him up to the top field.

The solitariness is what kept him living alone as a farmer. He relished his independence, which was another reason why he was still single. There had been women when he was younger, but nowadays he settled for lusting and fantasising over Delores.

The entrance to the field was a straight run, no gates. He pulled in and levelled the tractor into the edge of the area to be worked. Using the lever behind the seat he dropped the harrow down to the ground and with a roar of the engine drove on up the field. A smile on his face and music filling the cab, he went to work.

After a couple of hours and two more cassette changes, Fred noticed someone enter the field through the hedgerow on the road side.

'What's his bloody game?' He said aloud.

Last time someone stumbled on to Fred's land it was a poacher who'd wished he hadn't. He really lost his temper with that particular guy, Dan, the son of the local pub landlord. After beating him down and confiscating his shotgun and snares, he stripped him down to his underpants and took him to his father. Tied up on the back of his open backed Land Rover, he paraded him slowly through town bearing a placard saying 'Poacher'. He had a visit shortly after. Over a cup of tea and half a packet of biscuits with the constable, Fred had promised not to be quite so 'enthusiastic' over the punishment if there ever was next time.

He raised the harrow, slipped the tractor into rabbit gear and gunned it towards the trespasser with a belch of black smoke roar. As he neared the stumbling man his eyebrows raised.

'Dan Wilkins, come back for more have ya?' he said with a broad smile.

He pulled up twenty feet from the still approaching man. Leaving the engine ticking over in neutral he jumped down with the agility of a younger man. He strode towards him anger brewing.

He slowed up as he noticed something was wrong with Dan. His eyes were locked on him and he was tripping towards him in an uncoordinated manner. He was also drenched in blood. Fred stopped for a moment. Dan continued on, his blank expression becoming more of a snarl. Fred moved on quickly and punched Dan so hard in the face that it made his hand smart. He stepped back and shook his hand with a whistle through clenched teeth. Dan turned his head back and continued on like a rabid animal.

Fred jogged back to the tractor. From the rear of it he pulled a spare tow hitch. He held the six inch long lump of iron with a ball on one end like a hammer.

'I'm warning you Dan, back up or you're a dead man,' he spat.

Dan continued on. Fred swung the makeshift weapon and connected full on with Dans cheek. The man flew sideways onto the floor from the force of the blow. To Fred's horror he turned with a gargled growl. His face was concaved from below his left eye, his nose as if pressed against a sheet of glass. Confused, Fred threw the tow hitch into the cab and followed it slamming the door shut behind him just a Dan reached it.

'What the fuck.' Fred kept repeating as he ground the gears of the tractor. The engine roared as he pulled away, Dan still hammering on the door. He picked up speed and very soon the man lost his footing. The tractor barely bumped as its massive rear wheel passed over his squirming body.

Fred slew the steering over and stopped with a shudder. He selected neutral and stepped down quickly. What was left of Dan lay under the raised harrow. A two foot section in the middle of his body was flat, with a few indentations matching the tread pattern of the tyre. One arm lay flattened and useless by his side, the other reached up towards Fred, the battered face still forcing a snarl.

'There's just no getting rid of you is there you little shit.' Said Fred as he calmly operated the lever dropping the harrow down on what was left of the man. Its discs cut him into strips like a sliced loaf of bread.

Fred got back into the cab and fiddled with the dial of the radio. All he came across were government warnings about rioting caused by illness and reports of cannibalism countrywide.

He got down from the tractor again and this time disconnected the harrow leaving it on the mangled corpse. He got back in and drove away from the macabre scene. His mind was only on one thing, he had to get the love of his life, Delores, back to his house and safety.

7 HAVEN

He was sitting in the conservatory and could clearly see his children enjoying the summer sunshine in their modest back garden. His daughter bounced around on the trampoline, his son tried to coax the family dog into the paddling pool with the promise of a lick on his ice cream cone. He could see his wife preparing a salad at the table for their lunch. Jack settled back on his reclining chair thinking what a fantastic moment it was. The mortgage was almost paid, money in the bank and promotion on the cards. It was the most perfectly lazy Sunday afternoon in summer that he could ever have imagined.

Then ominous dark clouds rolled in as the ringing started. The vision dimmed as if he was being drawn away, kicking and screaming. The sunlight became increasingly dulled giving way to the ersatz glow of low power fluorescent tubes. As he awoke, the dream of a long lost past faded into a distant memory. He tried to cling to it as reality muscled in giving way to the realism of his drab and grubby room that had previously been a teacher's office before the apocalypse started.

'Perimeter breached Jack,' said the silhouette leaning through the doorway.

'Oh shit, here we go again.'

Jack shifted to a seated position on the metal framed single bed with a sigh and rubbed his eyes to dispel the last particles of sleep and the happy memories of times gone by. He ran his hand over his crew cut head and pushed his feet into his gortex combat boots by the bed. He was already fully dressed in black lightweights and matching long sleeved tee-shirt. In that current way of life it paid to be ready for anything, as everything more often than not did happen.

The World had changed and the hierarchy had shifted. Life was now a constant struggle for survival. The sickness, known commonly as the

Isaiah effect, had hit with such virulence that all in the UK and around the World were caught out. Due to a distinct lack of serious weaponry in this country things got out of control quickly.

The military were sorely under equipped because of budgetary cuts, and what services had remained intact were currently on tours overseas. By the time the authorities had totally lost control it was too late to call them back as the outbreak had become a pandemic. The soldiers were either already dead or out of contact.

As the lights went out across the globe, so too did communications. The survivors became ever decreasing pockets of resistance to the affected people, and as supplies dwindled the hordes grew ever larger.

Jack walked towards the door and picked up his utility web belt. It contained his pick axe and pistol holster and a few essential survival items which he stuffed in his large thigh pockets. Heading towards the corridor he pulled the webbing over his shoulders and clipped it around his waist. He grabbed his distressed leather jacket from the back of the door and picked up his Glock 17 pistol from the desk by the bed. He pulled back the slide chambering a round, and then thumbed on the safety before sliding it into the holster. Eight months earlier he'd never actually seen a gun in the flesh, let alone held one. He continued the short walk up the corridor and into the operations centre.

The ops centre, a converted gymnasium, had large tables which were clustered together in the middle and spread out with maps, photos and files. It wasn't dissimilar to the tables seen in old war movies, where WAF's in tight long line pencil skirts and white blouses pushed tiny models around a huge map to pin point positions of the enemy as well as friendly aircraft. The wooden exercise wall bars were also adorned with large maps plotted with crosses, stars and circles of varying marker pen colours. Around the tables was a bustle of activity with a great deal of toing and froing. Small groups of assorted people were in discussions casting occasional orders to others waiting at hand who turned to mark map's or collect other paperwork.

One person acknowledged the tough paramilitary looking Jack as he entered. The man turned awkwardly and with the use of a cane limped towards him. Shaddock was the head of this facility and on the whole was a good man. His background was one of politics but when the World went south he was one of the few that were practical enough to survive. He was at hand in parliament and sat in on most debates with regard to the spread of the effect. The rest of the government were more interested in the whys and how's. Shaddock's questions were 'what's the threat?' and 'how do we keep control when it gets out of hand?' Questions that were cast aside in parliamentary arguments that served no practical purpose. Shaddock was seen as a renegade and was ignored by his peers.

Unlike his associates in the house he continually argued that plans for Armageddon must be made, but he was generally laughed off the benches. This did not stop him making his own schemes and when the government shrank as MP's deserted their constituents and left the country, Shaddock sat tight and put his own plans into action. Although Jack admired him, he always felt Shaddock wasn't always telling all that he knew. After all, most politicians keep something under their hat with their non-committal theatrics.

'What's the score?' Jack said to the approaching man.

'There's been a little incursion by a handful of indigents,' he replied.

'Just call them Isaiah's like the rest of us Shaddock'

'Rogers was killed, they managed to find a weak spot in the fencing on the North side,' he said ignoring the sarcasm.

'It doesn't surprise me in the least, I've been warning engineering about that part of the fence rusting away for weeks.'

Light scattered gunfire could be heard outside causing them both to glance towards its general direction.

'Yes well, having been here as long as we have, the scavengers need to go further afield. As such they would much rather risk their lives for food and medicine than rolls of chain-link fencing,' was Shaddock's curt reply.

'Yeah, and keeping room for alcohol,' Jack spat under his breath.

'Pardon me?' Said Shaddock genuinely not hearing him.

'Oh nothing,' Jack replied dejectedly 'Where exactly did they get in?'

'Fourth section,' said Shaddock pointing to a schematic that lay out before him.

'Any other injuries?' queried Jack.

'Rogers is a fatality as I said. But as you know people tend not to be very vocal about injuries nowadays. As such we're not sure about the rest of his team at this present time'

'No problem, consider it sorted,' Jack abruptly replied. 'Okay, let's go.' He said to the two equally tough looking, but younger, men that now flanked him on either side. With that they turned and headed towards the double doors on the outer wall of the gym.

As the men walked out, the room had fallen silent apart from the three pairs of departing footsteps. Of all the jobs the New World order required, there in camp East 8 the killing crew was the most despised and feared by everyone.

Jack, Randal and Simon had found this place East 8, commonly known as Haven, when they had decided to venture out from the city. Although they came from different backgrounds they had become a tight group who made up a killing crew.

Simon was a jack the lad before the shit hit the fan, he was an East-end wide boy, had his fingers in many pies, including money laundering and selling moody items. He loved money but was too smart to knock off gas stations and bookies for the coins and kicks. He used his intelligence as a con man and entrepreneur, from which he made a comfortable living. Once people had started getting ill he even tried to profit from repackaging aspirin as a protective treatment. With things getting worse money became far less important, but due to his tough streetwise nature he survived on the street until he eventually hooked up with Randal and Jack.

Randal on the other hand was a bootboy. Not as bright and suave as Simon but he was twice as vicious. He had lived his life as far right wing as he could, even down to where his food came from, and had worked hard as a builder's labourer. He had loved his girlfriend and had only ever cried just once, for her.

Jack was the eldest of the crew, his training as a sales executive and his previous gym membership made him the obvious natural leader. Their experiences with the infection and general fitness made them all perfect for the crew, as it wasn't always the actual Isaiahs that needed to be despatched. There was absolutely no point in looking after those wounded by a bite or scratch from an assailant undergoing the Isaiah effect because infection rate was one hundred per cent, the few medicinal resources left were reserved for the uninfected that suffered everyday accidents and illnesses. Which meant if one became contaminated you would be either slaughtered on the spot or kicked out to take your chances in the open. More often than not you were just plain killed. Remorse had to be a forgotten concept.

The crew had been working together for about six months, and surviving together a little longer. Very few of the other survivors in East 8 had ever spoken to them. The bond between the three was strong and they trusted each other wholeheartedly. With every job they completed, their friendship and reliance on each other grew stronger.

The group's job was a simple one, as so many tasks appeared to be in this new world. They were judge, jury and above all executioner. If you had taken injury from one of the infected they would finish you without blinking - because a bite meant infection and infection meant the possibility of destroying their safe haven, and above all their own self-preservation was the biggest factor.

As far as the killing crew were concerned, there were only two types of people left in this world, the living and the dead. And they hated the effect because it had taken away all that was precious to them, lovers, parents and children. They hated the whole situation and especially detested the walking abominations that horded together and destroyed life irrespective of class, creed or colour.

8 INCURSION

They headed past the vegetable plots and on towards a lit up area of fence a couple of hundred yards ahead, the lights would only be used for a short time so as not to attract more. As they neared the small group they could see that they were locked in combat with a horde of around thirty infected. They had the upper hand as their attackers were uncoordinated and sluggish. They could see occasional muzzle flashes but most were battling hand to hand with all manner of weaponry.

The group were not seasoned zombie killers like themselves and very rarely left the compound unlike the crew who weren't keen on Shaddock's rules and regulations all of the time and tended to be self-governing. Shaddock knew the crew always had the best interests of the haven in mind and often turned a blind eye.

Looking over the combatants it was obvious they were tired and it was highly probable that some were injured.

Jack snapped his head left and right, a mutual sign to his comrades that they should flank him on both sides. As they neared the affray he drew his modified rock climbing pick-axe from his webbing and unclipped the clasp from his side arm.

'Melton, Is that you?' Said Jack to one of the fighting men catching his breath at the rear of the fracas.

'Who's that? Oh Jack,' came Melton's breathless reply. 'They got through, just couldn't stop them. We're mopping up now.'

'Has Rogers' body been dealt with?' Jack said sternly.

'Err, he's over there. Melton loosely pointed towards the edge of the fence a few yards away from the break. Jack walked over to the corpse laid out straight on the mud and unceremoniously pulled back the coat uncovering its face. As suspected they hadn't destroyed the brain. Rogers had been heavily mauled.

Jack had known Rogers, he'd been old school get down and dirty like him and had been one of the few survivors that he had a good rapport with. He understood the need for the crews job and accepted it, had he been a little younger he most probably would have been a crew member. Previously, before the country's collapse, he had also been in sales, as such the two of them had a lot in common. Jack knew Rogers would have been straight into the fight which would explain why his injuries were so severe. He'll be turning over in his grave, that he'd not yet been buried in, if he knew how they had left him. He was laid on his back, in the mud un-dealt with.

It would be a couple of hours before he re-animated, but the science wasn't an exact one. It could in fact be minutes.

This was an after effect of dying at the hands of Isaiah. They became the walking dead. The governments of the World conveniently omitted to make that public when it could still have been stopped, mainly because they didn't believe the fact themselves. As a result the cities had become a hotbed of the infection, the cause being the brains had not been destroyed in the bodies that were piled high in un-burnt pyres in the streets. Before long they reanimated and started to feed on anyone they could find.

Jack took his stance and buried the pick axe into Rogers's forehead, after prying the weapon free and wiping the tool on the bodies clothing, he replaced Rogers's jacket over his face. The men that stood nearby looked at him with disgust and fear in their eyes.

'Bury him,' he ordered.

'But we're supposed to burn them all,' said a young man as he passed him.

'Not him,' he spat out. 'Bury him with respect.'

Randal and Simon had joined the battle. Skilfully they beheaded and disabled corpse after corpse their energy strong as the other group waned. Randal stabbed and skewered with his favoured stiletto style dagger penetrating brainstems left and right, he preferred the personal approach. Simon was less refined with his machete hacking limb, head and spine. Despite their brutal fighting they kept half an eye on Jack ready to back him up if required, peripheral vision was a godsend.

Jack headed back towards Melton. On his way he noted a further half a dozen freshly dead fighters laid out behind them.

'For Christ's sake mate, how many have you lost?' He said motioning towards the laid out bodies. Melton's body language shouted the worst. 'Are you injured?'

He stammered 'No, God no. Just a scratch from when the fence came down.'

Gripping Melton's arm Jack said 'Show me.'

'It's nothing, I'm not lying,' he began to plead.

Jack slipped the pick into his belt and grabbed Melton pulling his jacket from around his neck. One of Melton's team stepped forward but was stopped in his tracks as Randal grabbed him brandishing his knife.

'I don't think you'll be wanting to do that,' he whispered threateningly into his ear.

Jack could clearly see the ring of indentations indicating a human bite mark on Melton's neck, not deep, but enough to pierce the skin in a couple of places, which is all that was needed for Isaiah to take effect. Slipping his foot behind Melton's he tripped him and pushed him backwards, as he dropped heavily on to his back, Jack whipped the pick from his belt and before Melton had registered imminent death was on its way he was on the floor. The weapon pierced his skull with a hammer blow snuffing his life in an instant.

Jack unceremoniously levered the pick from his head as Randal released the now passive man, some more of Melton's associates eyed the crew even more suspiciously.

Jack addressed the group 'If you ain't got a scratch from these pusbags then you have nothing to worry about. Let's get this place secure.'

Melton's men under the leadership of Jack's crew managed to fend back and deplete the undead. In the last few minutes of the melee a young man approached Jack from behind. Jack knew his name was Gant and had often seen him leaving Melton's room late at night.

Gant sped up as he got closer. It was as if Jack had eyes in the back of his head. Just before Gant made contact, he ducked down. This action revealed Randal's crooked smile and the youth ploughed straight into the cold steel of his blade.

'You really shouldn't have tried that,' he said to him 'You didn't give me time to clean my knife. You're as dead as your boyfriend now.'

He raised his boot and kicked him off his weapon. Gant landed on his back in the mud desperately clutching the stomach wound, blood filtered in rivulets through his fingers. Fear turned to panic. Simon stood over him.

'Night, night,' Simon said.

Gants cry of 'no' was cut short as Simon beheaded him with a single blow from his machete.

As the fight ended Jack dealt with the bodies of the unlucky fighters that fell in the brief battle, his accomplices checked over the survivors for injuries. Some were open and showed them their lack of injury, whereas others were just plain awkward despite being uninjured themselves. They all knew the rules of East 8 and the risk if even one infected person was allowed to stay within the compound. But this didn't stop people detesting the killing crew, especially so after the incident with Melton and Gant. Jack, Randal and Simon could see the hate in the eyes of the men they'd just fought beside. It just confirmed to the crew that these guys had been sheltered for too long at what was going on outside the fences.

Heading back to the complex the mood was frosty between the two groups. The crew allowed Melton's men to go through the main doors preferring not to have them following up behind. The last one past stopped and stared angrily into Jack's face.

'You'll go to Hell you evil Bastard,' then carried on into the complex.

'From what I've seen we're already living in it,' Jack said following on.

Jack, holding the door open, stopped and looked into the bemused faces of Simon and Randal and said 'I think it might be time for a recon road trip.' Simon smirked and they both nodded in agreement. They often left for a few days after an altercation, not just to clear their heads, but also to avoid the pointless paperwork and questions that Shaddock would fire at them. It's always tough when members of the survivors succumbed and had to be despatched, but they felt questions might be asked about the demise of Gant.

They felt no remorse at what they had just done, self-preservation was essential to survive, on the whole and as a unit.

9 EXCURSION

Early the following morning, the crew were at the prefabricated garage area in their small workshop that they had created between a couple of ex-military utility vehicles. They were preparing their cycles for their trip. They preferred to travel by bicycle. It was a quiet way to travel and top specification mountain bikes were easy to find and comfortable enough for long distances. Also, of course, the only fuel is human strength and endurance. Petrol had long since gone stale or evaporated from most vehicles. Diesel fared better but the noise was prohibitive, a vehicle would end up being a pied piper in a quiet World without even ambient sound. They only used powered transport when absolutely necessary.

Randal often commented that the only person who could afford to buy one of the top notch bikes that they used was the rich Executive who was too overweight and unfit to ride it. They strapped on luggage in the form of side panniers and handlebar packs. The lightweight military style clothing they wore was perfect for comfortable riding, and hi-tech gel seats made the ride all the more serene and comfortable. They carried a few MRE's, emergency medical supplies, maps and their weapons, together with other survival aids such as water purification tablets and petrol conditioner. Some space was reserved for items they might scavenge. Most essential of all they had two water bottles each in carriers connected to the frames.

When they eventually rode away from safe haven the only wave they received was the wave of relief over the rest of the survivors that they had departed, some wishing they'd never come back.

They rode out through the main gates at the crack of dawn. The sun was just making its appearance over the horizon to welcome in the new day. The guard protecting the entrance had opened up one side of the chain link gate and swung it wide as they approached. This was the only acknowledgement he made of their existence, his eyes still scanning the roadway ever vigilant.

Out in the countryside they would only see the occasional walking corpse and never really more than a pair. By the time the dead noticed them they had already peddled past and were many tens of yards away the only noise from their well-oiled bikes being the friction between the tyres and asphalt. The undead would sometimes trail after them for a while until their attention was drawn elsewhere or they just forgot what they were walking towards in the first place.

These little jaunts were more for the members of the crews' own rest and recuperation than any reconnaissance to help the folks at East 8, sometimes it was safer on the outside. It was rare they went back without any important information or essential medical supplies. For sure, East 8 was a secure place to be with the other survivors and structure that prevented anarchy. But when it came down to it the nature of their tasks separated them from their peers on a trusting level and they had to watch their backs almost all the time. The incident with Melton and Gant was a good example, and not the first.

It was quite ironic that they felt safer outside the gates of the camp. Knowing they were hated made them more careful and paranoia was a helpful trait.

'Fancy a break Jack?' said Simon.

'Not really but it sounds like you do,' he laughed.

Jack pulled up at a wide verge in the open lane they had been travelling along. He took a few small sips from his water bottle, enough to quench his thirst but too little to cause a stitch, hydration was important, but over hydration was deadly.

'What's the score then boss?' asked Randal.

'Not really going anywhere in particular. We're just keeping an eye out for anything of interest.'

'I say fine. Just happy to be out of that place for a while,' Randal replied motioning back the way they had come.

'Don't be hard on them brother,' Simon joined. 'They just don't have the guts to do what we have to.'

'They got the same guts as us when those fuckers are hungry. They're just living to die.' Randal replied. Simon snorted at the comment.

'Yeah well, maybe we should get moving. We'll turn off just up the road. Start looking for somewhere secure to rest up for the night.'

They re-mounted their bikes and carried on deeper into the peaceful countryside. They had travelled this way many times before. The infected were few and far between in the area. Pickings were also slim, being within thirty or so miles of the camp. The area had been looted many times over. Jack turned into a smaller lane they had not travelled down before. It was relatively clear of abandoned traffic unlike the roads close to larger towns. The vehicles sat in hedgerows and left in the road in the current area were more likely to be the much more functional four wheel drive variety as opposed to the comparatively useless compact hybrids found in the cities. The vehicles found out of town also tended to be diesel. If they needed to escape fast it was so much easier in the country with its wide open spaces and very little habitation.

Before long they came across a not so lonely row of houses in the middle of nowhere. Not so lonely due to the fact that there was a reasonably sized group of infected gathered at the front of the end house. They had the uncanny ability of sensing where survivors were holed up. The crew pulled up a few hundred yards short and stood in a line across the narrow lane.

'What do you think?' said Jack reaching back for the rifle scope in the pannier of his bike.

'Must be survivors,' Simon replied. The row was four houses linked in pairs with garages attached to each one, the middle garages attached. Typical of the houses built in the sixties and seventies. The style usually had three bedrooms and a bathroom on the first floor with kitchen, diner and lounge on the ground floor. Jack imagined the rooms with high ceilings and the décor to have garish wallpaper remembering back to his grandparents' house as a child. These houses were almost identical. The house at the nearest end to them appeared to be the focus of the hordes attention.

'Okay who's turn is it to run decoy? I want to have a look inside and hopefully the occupants will still be on our side.'

Moving his bike to the side of the road he retrieved his webbing and sidearm, as too did his associates.

'I'll go,' Randal offered still standing astride his bike.

'Are you sure?' Jack said.

'Well there's no way you're going to get in without a diversion of some kind. There must be seventy to eighty of those things down there.'

Randal was right, they almost completely surrounded the house two to four deep in places. They pawed at the conveniently boarded up lower windows.

'Anyway, I ain't the most diplomatic of people they see my ugly mug and they'll run for the hills.' They all laughed. Jack offered his hand. Randal shook it firmly.

'Good luck my friend. We'll see you back in a couple of hours,' Jack said. Randal turned to Simon and they also shook hands.

'Give them hell brother,' he said.

'Okay then, let's do it,' said Randal.

He got on his bike and after a quick 'so long' he peddled down the road towards the horde. The other two left their bikes and continued slowly on foot in the same direction. At the distance they were away from the animalistic group they wouldn't suspect them to be warm meat. They stopped for a moment and watched Randal as he peddled hard towards the houses.

'He's such a nutter, I'm sure it was my turn.' Simon smiled.

'I never keep track, but he's right. Imagine waiting for your knight in shining armour and he pops his skinhead in the door.' Jack smiled.

'Ah, God bless 'im.' Replied Simon.

10 DIVERSION

Randal headed quickly towards the group of Isaiah's that surrounded the house. He detected the sickly odour of decay pervading his nose and mouth and retched slightly in disgust. Some of them turned their heads and bodies to view the spritely moving object.

As he got nearer a domino effect occurred, causing more and more of the infected to turn and notice him. He passed the group and shouted 'Come and get some fast food.' This gave the outermost the impetus to follow this obviously healthy person. As the journey continued Randal occasionally slowed and sped up again cat-calling to keep the group interested and following.

After a quarter of an hour or so he assumed the guys would have gained entry to the house by that time, he pedalled harder and changed up a gear with a dull clicking of the selector. As he made headway the horde tripped and stumbled to keep up, but distance was being gained.

As the road sloped he stopped peddling allowing the downward momentum to carry him with much less effort. The road at the bottom of the hill turned sharply around a bend with his vision obscured on either side by thick hedgerows. He angled the bike at speed to allow him to corner quickly and get out of sight. As he rounded the bend the road straightened out again allowing him to see further forward. For a split second he held his breath, thinking fast he steered the bike harder to avoid hitting the stationary agricultural tractor blocking half the road.

Unfortunately his actions were still a little too late as he clipped the unprotected front wheel of the leviathan. His bicycle was viciously tossed aside as Randal was launched into the air. Having no control over his trajectory his arms flailed and he landed hard onto an aged pile of dead and decomposing bodies by the side of the road. He rolled off the stinking heap having lost momentum and rolled onto his back with the wind knocked out of him and a sharp agonizing pain in the side of his lower abdomen.

He ignored the shock and attempted to rise knowing the pack wouldn't be too far behind him. He tried to sit up straight which caused a throbbing pain to rake down his side. He felt dampness and before he even looked he knew he was seriously injured.

He inspected the wound and the sight that met his eyes caused him to yelp. He had been impaled by a thin rib bone from one of the desiccated corpses that broke his landing. He immediately grabbed it and with a blood curdling scream he yanked the bone from his stomach and threw it aside. Although bleeding profusely from the possibly infected wound. He managed to get to his feet as the sounds of the moans and scuffles of the approaching horde reached his ears. He limped holding his side, over to the twisted metal that used to be his bike. He pulled free the saddlebags and headed for the cab of the tractor. The door swung wide as he pulled at the handle. He managed to crawl into the cab and lock himself in as the first of the horde reached his hiding place. He was secure in the cab, but visible, the doors rattled with the slapping blows of the corpses.

He managed to stop the bleeding and patch up the wound quickly and was feeling the benefits of the pain killers he had poured down his neck from the bottle in his bag. The aggressive horde clamoured to get into the tractor and their quarry, he sat back contemplating his next move as the cabin vibrated and rattled around him.

Whilst he sat recuperating he noticed a rabbits foot swaying with the motion of the cab, it dangled down from the steering column. He leant forward to take a closer look. A bunch of keys hung from the ignition of the tractor.

'No way!' he exclaimed.

He turned the key to the first position, the dash board instantly lit up and the stereo blared out some classical style music from the twin speakers making him jump. He reached up and turned the volume down on the antiquated cassette radio fitted to the front of the ceiling. He listened for a few seconds, he tried to remember the last time he actually heard music. Making sure the transmission was in neutral he flicked the key further and after a short amount of turning the engine roared into life belching thick black smoke up from the funnel out front.

'God bless diesel,' he laughed.

He depressed the heavy clutch pedal which further aggravated his stomach injury, and with some grinding he selected first gear. Releasing the clutch he gently accelerated, the tractor jolted and lurched. The undead were jostled and jolted as the monstrous rear tyres bumped into them back and forth. It had been many years since Randal had driven agricultural tractors, the occasional small digger on sites, but the full size thing had been something from his teenage summer harvests earning pocket money in his home village.

Gaining forward motion the giant wheels turned, the heavy tread pattern grabbed at the nearest of the dead and dragged them down to become a pulpy mess beneath. He drove away from the direction he had come and steered the vehicle left and right to obliterate more of the pursuing creatures. He did this with immense pleasure until the horde was no more than a gooey mess all-over the road. Up ahead he could see a farmhouse, not wanting to lead any stragglers back to his friends he headed toward it. If he could get inside without being seen he could hide up till after dark and head back without leading the dead back.

As he neared the farmhouse he could see that someone had clearly scrawled the word 'Keep Out' across the fascia above the upper windows. Randal slowed the tractor and turned into the driveway, he scanned around then jumped down from the cab with a wince almost forgetting about his injury thanks to the light headedness caused by the pharmaceuticals.

The driveway up to the house was blocked by a chest high metal gate, thankfully it was not locked and he unlatched it swinging it wide. He scanned around yet again but there were no cadavers around. He got back into the idling tractor and pulled through the entrance, he shut off the engine and got down again then closed the gate behind him, it wasn't much protection from a horde but could well slow them up enough to gain valuable seconds.

Randal hobbled up the track to the porch covered side door of the farmhouse. On reaching it he tried the handle finding it locked. He rapped on the door vigorously. He peeked through the letterbox but could only see darkness. Then for a split second he saw a dull glow against the shadows moving somewhere in the rear of the house.

'Hey. Let me in. I'm a survivor,' he called into the house. He was answered by a sudden movement as two hollow tubes of a twelve gauge shotgun almost hit him in the face as it was pushed out.

'Whoa, there's no need for that,' he said

'Go away. I don't want anyone in my house. You're trespassing.' The deep voice answered from the opposite side of the door.

'I just want to rest up for a while, and I'll be gone. That's all.'

'No,' came the firm reply.

Randal heard the double click of the hammers being drawn back on the archaic firearm.

'I'll give you to the count of three, and if you're not gone I'll blow your bloody head off.'

Randal gathered himself. He had to get inside otherwise he would have no chance to get back to the others safely. There was an open barn opposite but no cover apart from a battered Land Rover and a vintage looking open tractor to the side. All he would achieve by running straight back would be leading the horde back to them. He needed to lie low and let the horde dissipate.

'One'

He picked up his pack but remained in front of the door. This guy was playing hard ball.

'Look I'm not asking for supplies or anything, I just need to rest up till the infected bog off.'

'Two'

Randal was tired and weak. He looked back to see a dozen or so Isaiah's had already gathered at the gate. He desperately needed to get out of sight. If this unknown man had to die to facilitate it then so be it. It was kill or die.

'Three'

Randal shoved his bag on the end of the barrels and pushed just as both hammers dropped.

The percussion caps triggered on both cartridges simultaneously. The force expelled the lead shot in forward motion. The space between it and the blockage became highly pressurized seeking the weakest part of the weapon to break out. It did, with an ear-splitting boom.

Randal was thrown back. The contents of his damaged saddle bag fell to the floor. He was briefly deafened.

The letter box had become a misshapen ragged hole. He acted fast and tentatively he put his hand through into the dark void through the hole. He scrabbled about for a few seconds and unlatched the lock. It was stiff to push having been blocked by the body of his assailant.

When he had room to enter he pulled a small torch from the hip pocket of his combats. The light breeze of the open door blew the cordite smell and smoke away in swirls. He stepped into the kitchen of the cottage. He swung the torch around to check he was safe. He caught sight of a battery powered lantern on the table. He flicked it on bathing the room in a strong fluorescent glow. It was messy but not unhealthily so with clean and dirty crockery on the worktop, and well stocked cupboards on the walls.

Randal gathered up his fallen items quickly from the step and mat. The gate behind the tractor was now teeming with undead attracted by the exploding gun and it was beginning to bend under the pressure. He stepped back inside, closed and locked the door. He inspected the body behind it. The man had been big, not fat but very tall and broad. His hair was long and unkempt, as was his bushy grey beard.

The only irregularity was the angular shard of gunmetal protruding from his right eye socket. Despite having only just died he stank worse than one of the corpses outside. He turned away wafting the stink from his face.

He took the lamp from the table and prepared to investigate the rest of the house. He pulled his pistol from its holster. If there were more survivors they wouldn't be very happy that he had already slaughtered one of their number. Movement from upstairs forced him into action. He paused as a wave of nausea swept over him, his mouth became dry and he had to lean against the door. It passed and he continued his check of the ground floor.

More rumbles were heard from above as he reached a staircase. Lamp and gun held ahead he crept up the stairs. The landing was dark apart from occasional thin slivers of light from gaps where the boards met covering the windows. The first room was empty apart from a soiled camp bed and assorted clothes lying around.

He moved out of the room and approached the next door. He placed the lamp on the floor and holding the gun ahead he opened and pushed the door hard. It swung open and slammed against the wall. He relaxed slightly when the source of the noise was confirmed.

The figure that was tied spread eagled to the bed was dead. She looked at him through white eyes and a toothless mouth gaped at his entrance. In life this woman was probably quite beautiful, but in death her naked body was ravaged with stale decay. Her long blond hair was matted and unkempt. Tell-tale marks revealed what the man downstairs had been up to for who knows how long. Randal was disgusted. He raised his pistol and dispatched the zombie immediately. After checking the rest of the upper floor he headed back downstairs.

He was exhausted as he collapsed into a stained comfy chair in the sitting room. It was positioned so he had a good view of the back door. Through the hole he could see the dead beyond trying to get at him. As the day turned to night he was itching to get away from this evil place and back to his friends.

He felt bad, really bad. To start with he thought he had overdosed on the strong painkillers he had downed earlier, but now he was thinking the worst. He felt cold and hot at the same time, he had become infected by the injury. He sobbed as he unlatched the door, he was going to make a run for it and take out as many of the abominations as he could. He pulled open the door and stepped into the quickly darkening evening. The undead ignored him. It was as if they could sense he was fast becoming one of them. He raised his hand to shoot the nearest. But his gun was gone. His vision was dull his hearing almost non-existent. Walking was an effort he felt so stiff and jerky. He repeated in his head,

'Must meet up with Jack and Simon' which degenerated into

'Must meet Jack Simon' and the penultimate thought

'Meet Jack Simon' and then lastly

'Meat' Randal died as he left the house, and he now headed back to the last place he instinctively knew that there was warm flesh.

11 DISCOVERY

As Jack and Simon neared the houses only a handful of the Isaiah's remained. Further on down the lane the rest had ambled out of sight chasing after Randal. They had used that particular ruse a few times and it was usually at least a couple of hours before they regrouped. Their priority now was to get inside and assess the situation. They fanned out as they approached. Jack was at the ready with his pick and Simon was brandishing his machete. The infected people that were still close to the house seemed to be in poor condition. Some were not even aware as the pick or machete ended their last vestige of imitation living.

The downstairs windows and doors were boarded up tight. It looked as if the house had been so since before the outbreak, possibly an eviction or repossession. In an upstairs room Jack caught a brief glimpse of a woman's face looking down at them through a grimy window. An upstairs window opened and they were pleased to see a rope ladder descending from it.

Jack motioned Simon up the ladder whilst he kept watch at the bottom. He glanced up to see Simon's foot disappear inside then he climbed up. He pulled himself through the window as three more undead had gathered below. It wouldn't take long for more to appear but for the moment they were secure. Jack pulled the ladder up behind him then closed the window.

He turned and greeted the woman who had allowed them entry into the house.

'Hello there, my names Jack and this is Simon,' Simon smiled nodding politely to the unkempt woman.

'I'm Sarah,' she replied. Jack scanned the gloomy room, the smell inside was a mixture of food, stale sweat and sewage, not overpowering but apparent.

'How long have you been hiding out here?' he asked her.

'Not long, probably a couple of weeks. We escaped from a camp about ten miles from here. It was overrun,' Sarah said obviously a little distraught at the recollection. Simon interjected 'You said we. Is there more of you here?'

'There are three of us, myself and my two girls.' She led them out of the room down the stairs and towards what used to be the kitchen at the back of the house. She halted and turned to Jack,

'Please be gentle, the girls are still quite traumatized.'

'It's okay I have, I mean had two children myself.' He trailed off as unwanted memories came to the fore.

Two camping gas lamps effectively lit the room. Huddled together in a cot to the side of the room were two children, the younger one cuddling a black stuffed cat. Wide eyes gazed out at the two warriors.

'How's your food situation?' Jack said as he turned to Sarah.

'Not good, I've been rationing what little we have, the girls are so weak and hungry.'

'Not to worry, one of us will nip back to the bikes after dark. We have plenty of dehydrated iron rations. Then we'll think about taking you back to East 8 with us. Hopefully Randal will be back after dark too. How's your water situation?'

'I filled up everything I could find, the water only went off a few days ago. So I drained all the hot water tanks here and next door. I've been boiling it to be on the safe side.'

'That was a very smart thing to do,' he said admiringly.

Looking at the children's thousand yard stare and obviously suffering from a little malnutrition weakened Jack's stony heart bringing back his own loss, he needed to help them for his own peace of mind. The girls were six and eight years old, slightly younger than his own children had been. Hopefully they would come through the mess that the world had become, and be a stronger next generation for it.

Their mother had been doing a fantastic job of looking after them but their resources and time had pretty much run out. Jack suspected they wouldn't have lasted another week if they hadn't turned up.

'Was it the North Dene refugee camp you were staying at?' Jack queried.

'Yes it was, do you know about it?' Sarah asked.

'We were there last week, it was a mess. Looked to us like the forces bugged out at the first sign of trouble,' said Jack.

'Wasn't anything to scavenge either, looks like the place was pretty much out of supplies,' added Simon.

'It was harsh,' she grimaced, 'it was fine when we first got there. It was like being at a holiday camp. But then they came.' She motioned a hand to the window 'Everyday there were more and more, the truck supplies stopped and the rationing was becoming a serious problem. A week after the supplies stopped coming half the soldiers were gone.'

'Sounds about right, we weren't to know how long the place had been empty. It looks like we were only a few days too late,' Jack said.

'It was the soldiers fault. They were so busy fighting amongst themselves they hadn't noticed that the fences were starting to fail. Then one day they just collapsed down one side due to the weight of bodies pushing against them.' Her eyes watered as she recollected it. 'They came in so fast, ripping and tearing at the people who were just too shocked or too frail to move. I grabbed the girls and locked ourselves in one of the portable toilet cubicles. The hardest thing was to keep the girls quiet. We spent the whole night inside that rotten stinking toilet. It wasn't until I hadn't heard a single noise for what seemed like hours before we stepped out of that cubicle.'

'My god, how did you make it here?' Simon asked.

'It was more luck than judgement. We just walked across fields, keeping away from roads and villages. Then we eventually came across a farmhouse just down the road. There was a strange man there, he refused to let us in but did tell us about these houses. To be honest there was something a bit odd about him. I wouldn't have felt safe staying with him.'

'Do you think he's still there?' said Jack.

'Probably, he was well boarded up. He said it was his farm, so he'd probably been there all his life.'

'Might be worth checking him out, a survivor is another soldier on our side,' said Simon.

'We'll call on him, it'll be a couple of days before we can move out anyway.' agreed Jack. 'You've had it pretty damn tough,' he said turning his conversation back to Sarah.

Simon went back to making daft faces at the girls. The younger of the two girls showed signs of a smile forming at the edges of her mouth. She still kept snuggled up to her toy cat for comfort. That was a good sign.

'What's this camp East 8 like?' Sarah queried.

'It's a little officious but it's safe. The place itself is made up of what used to be quite a sprawling school. With the help of a government minister it was set up in the early days of the epidemic. Simon, Randal and I left the city and stumbled upon it by chance.'

'Well it sounds like a safer place than here,' she replied.

They all relocated to an upstairs room that the three survivors were using as a bedroom. Sarah and the girls cuddled up together on the mattress to get some well-earned sleep, something Sarah had been lacking. Now she had protection sleep came much easier.

Jack and Simon left them to get some rest and headed through to the front bedroom to keep a lookout for Randal. Simon leaned on the window sill and looked out at the countryside and road below.

'It's been three hours, I really expected him back by now,' he said.

'I know, let's not give up hope just yet,' replied Jack as he joined him at the window.

12 NIGHTSHIFT

It had been about an hour after dark when Jack and Simon decided to head back to the bikes and the essential supplies they held. They walked into the unused small back bedroom. Jack looked over the improvised rope ladder. He was impressed. The treads were fashioned from the struts of the staircase and the rope had been made by tightly winding sheets and tying them together. Sarah had done a good job. Despite looking lost and nervous he suspected her to be a strong survivor when it counted, after all she had kept the three of them alive throughout this mess single handed.

He opened the window wide allowing the cool fresh air to flood in, pushing the stuffiness of the closed up house back out of the room. Jack leant out of the window. It was a clear night lit by an almost full moon. Behind the house only four of the abominations seemed present and were well spread out.

As quietly as possible he lowered the ladder. When it reached level with the tops of the downstairs windows he whispered,

'Okay.'

Simon took over and tied off the ladder tightly to the long defunct central heating pipes. Jack leaned towards him,

'I've let the ladder down to about six feet from the floor. Hopefully none of the pusbags will be able to snag it or pull it down.'

'Good thinking boss. Don't really want to get stuck down there, especially when it's nice and secure up here,' Simon replied.

Jack threw his leg over the window sill and quietly descended. He reached the end of the ladder and let his feet dangle as he utilized his upper body strength and used his arms to climb down the rest of the way until his feet hit the floor.

With his back to the wall he surveyed the rear garden. It was a modest lawn with what used to be flowerbeds running along both sides. There were two infected nearby.

Against the house, under the protection of the dark shadows neither one had noticed him. Simon joined him underneath the ladder and looked over at him. It was a clear night and he understood the hand signal Jack had given him. He silently drew his machete as Jack readied his pick.

They broke from each other heading in opposite directions along the dark edge of the house. Like a well-choreographed dance routine they both circled around taking the infected by surprise. They both swung their weapons in unison, connecting with their individual targets. Within seconds the two threats were eliminated.

Even though there was very little sound during the covert attack on the two Isaiah's, there was enough to interest the other two who were previously loitering on the other side of the fenceless barrier between the garden and the rear track.

During their many bouts with the infected over the past months, the crew had managed to devise tactics when dealing with them. They were predictable in their patterns taking the straightest route to reach their prey. Small groups were easy to outsmart. When dealing with larger hordes it was much more difficult due to their resilience. Humans tire the infected keep on going, albeit slowly. In that situation you get up high and prey they dissipate before you die of dehydration or starvation.

Silence was the key, in the dark their eyesight was next to useless.

In similar fashion to disposing of the previous two they circled round. Jack pick-axed one through the face and Simon hefted the machete above his head and striking hard cleaved the skull of the other into two halves.

After they had wiped their weapons down on the cadavers clothing they re-holstered them and moved with stealth along the track which led them up to the road. By the time they hit it they were far enough away from the front of the house as not to attract the attentions of the undead there.

A figure stumbled in the same direction ahead of them. They approached it silently from the shadows. Something seemed familiar, this corpse was fresh. It only walked with the supplest of limps and if it wasn't for the tilted head in the darkness this individual could look alive. Jack gripped Simons shoulder, he held up a finger in Simons face. He stood still as Jack continued on. He pulled the ice axe from his belt as he closed in he said,

'Hey!' and flicked on his penlight briefly.

The figure turned suddenly and he looked into the ravaged face of Randal. Simon noticeably sighed a few feet behind him. On seeing him, Randal's mouth turned to a snarl, lips peeled back and he launched at him.

'Sorry mate,' Jack said as he plunged the ice axe point first through Randal's eye and deeper on into the brain, immediately de-animating the body of his friend.

He stood silently in the darkness over the crumpled body of his friend and team mate as Simon stepped up to his side. Jack held the pick loosely by his side and took in the peacefulness of the night. After a few minutes he placed the pick in his belt and picked up Randal under the arms as Simon took his feet. They dragged him over to the verge. Once they had placed him as respectfully as they could Jack went through his pockets for anything they may need. His pistol was missing, as was his pack, but he did find a half box of nine mil shells and his signature stiletto dagger. He turned it in his hand thinking back to the times when this man had backed him up and saved his life on more than one occasion.

He remembered back to when they had first met. Jack had been psychotic and reckless towards the infected. He had just wanted them all dead. In their time they had killed many hundreds, possibly even thousands of them.

The last item he recovered was Randal's wallet. He flicked it open and was greeted by the face of a pretty blond girl. He looked at it thoughtfully in the shaded pen light glow. A sigh escaped his lips as he closed the wallet and placed it into the breast pocket of Randal's jacket.

'Time to rest, buddy,' he said in a whisper, 'I hope you find her on the other side.'

Thankfully there were no others nearby. The bikes were still right where they had been left earlier in the day. They mounted them and rode slowly back down towards the houses. They avoided free-wheeling as the clicking of the gears would be easily heard. They slowly came to a stop as they reached the entrance to the rear track, preferring to walk the last short stretch with the bikes on their shoulders.

The back of the house was still clear. They leaned the bikes against the wall. Beside the house was a one car sized garage which was empty, adjoining it was the neighbours. From their current position at the back they had access to the rear door of it. Simon stood at the ready as Jack tried the handle, it was open. He pushed the door open with his own pick at the ready. He entered carefully ensuring his small torch was shaded.

Against the back wall was a small workbench with a few hand tools, the shelves above which held jars and receptacles holding all manner of fastening. The majority of the space was taken up by a dusty but well looked after compact car. He went back to the other garage and motioned for Simon to wheel the bikes in. He wheeled the first through the doorway, Jack took it and leaned it against the wall, and then he unbuckled the panniers and packs. Simon wheeled the other bike in and Jack took the handle bars handing the packs from the first to Simon. He positioned the second bike next to the first and removed the luggage from it also.

They exited the garage and stood under the ladder. They tied the packs to the last rung and one by one they climbed back up finally pulling up the packs through the window.

They were relieved to be back in the safety of the house. They had some serious things to talk about, Sarah was up and about and the girls were still asleep. Over some freeze dried coffee they discussed and drew up a plan of action.

They needed transport. It was possible the car they found earlier in the next door garage was usable. That would be Simons job, he could hotwire cars better than Jack.

Both of them would check out the farmer the next morning. It seemed he was probably sorted to survive alone. Jack's sense of compassion felt he had to check, just in case the guy would be happy under a government umbrella of protection.

If all went well, they would either return to the house with the farmer or pick him up the day after and head back to East 8. Someone knowledgeable in horticulture would be a valuable asset to take back with them.

A couple of days should be enough for the girls and Sarah to get their strength back enough to travel. Despite the journey not being too far, plans do have a habit of having to be altered ad hoc. As such Jack wanted them fit enough for any eventuality.

13 VISITING

It was shaping up to be a drizzly morning. That was a good thing. The rain masked a lot of sound, and any noise they made wouldn't carry very far at all. From the information Sarah had given them they were looking for a farmhouse just off the road with all its windows boarded up. There was a tractor half blocking the road before they'd get to it with a few infected rotting corpses by the vehicle.

The plans had been made the previous night after they had recovered their bicycles and dealt with their friend. They would call on the farmer today, after their return Simon was going to have a closer look at the car in the neighbouring garage, even though it was petrol driven they had an additive that would revive stale fuel, it was something they carried for situations such as this. The day after next they would be returning to East 8.

'Hey brother,' Simon said from behind him at the window.

Jack stopped azing out and turned with a smile,

'Morning, how are you doing?'

'Yeah good, missing Randal.'

'We know this guy turned Sarah and the girls away, makes you wonder why,' Jack said.

'Morning guys,' said Sarah from the doorway.

'Good Morning,' they chimed in unison.

She was happy to have adult company and keen to get herself and her daughters away from the tomb they currently resided in.

'I'm going to cook up some breakfast, do either of you want anything?' she asked.

'No we're absolutely fine, we're not breakfast people,' Jack said.

'Since macky dee's went the way of the world, I'd only miss my breakfast muffins even more if I had it,' grinned Simon.

With a smile on her face Sarah went back to the room she shared with the girls to get them downstairs. The men walked through to the small room they had used to exit and re-enter the house the night before. They looked out of the window. The four inert bodies lay in the early morning dew. No others had replaced them. The rear of the house was clear.

'Taking the bikes or walking?' said Simon as he gazed into the middle distance.

'It doesn't sound too far, easier to avoid trouble on foot,' replied Jack.

They headed downstairs. Sarah was preparing one of the ration packs and pouring water from a drinking bottle into a billy can on the gas stove. The girls were sat at the table drinking water from plastic beakers. Sally looked up and smiled as Simon walked in, he had a gift with girls of all ages thought Jack. He looked at the pair. Despite being a little grubby these angelic little girls gave him hope. He realised that these girls were part of the next generation, and they needed to be protected at all costs.

'Are you all right?' Sarah said immediately snapping him back from his thoughts.

'Yes sorry, I was miles away,' he said 'We're off to check on this neighbour of yours. We'll probably be gone for a few hours, please don't worry, we will come back for you.'

'I hope so, I really don't want us stuck here. For the girls sake I want to get away,' she said quietly out of earshot of the children.

'We'll check out this guy and if he's up for it we'll bring him back with us and we'll all go on back to East 8 together. I promise.'

Sarah felt comfortable with Jacks reply. The way he emphasised his last few words were obviously from the heart.

They said goodbye and headed back to the small bedroom. The rope ladder was still tied off to the pipes from the previous night. Jack opened the window and lowered it.

'Ready?' he said looking back to Simon.

'As ever, no.' Simon replied.

As quietly as possible Jack threw his leg over the sill and descended to the ground. He moved to the side to make room for Simon's descent. He drew his Glock and checked a round was chambered. They preferred the hand weapons but relied on pistols as a last resort. He slid the gun back into the holster as Simon finished checking his own.

They headed past the inanimate corpses. On reaching the track they headed the opposite way this time meeting the road on the far side of the row of houses. They came out closer to the front of their house. The horde was much smaller and they were of very little threat now. They stuck to the edge of the lane using the bordering hedgerow as cover. The condition of the paving on the road was still very good, the less travelled roads had very little in the way of abandoned vehicles and other detritus.

The morning had become clearer as the sun rose higher in the sky. They were offered no resistance as the infected were now few and far between. They picked up pace a little as the road sloped down towards a bend a few hundred yards further on. They approached the turn at its widest point cautiously. They edged round it and saw that the track levelled out. Ahead of them was more rubbish strewn out on the road than they had seen on the rest of the short journey put together.

They neared the piles of dirty soil coloured trash. Then realisation dawned on them, these were bodies, inanimate corpses. They scanned through the heaps, the majority were long dead. Some bore the signs of being crushed and mashed into the road. There was half a torso here and a pair of detached legs there.

'Here boss,' said Simon from the opposite side of the lane.

'What have you got?' he said as he headed over to his position.

"Randal's bike,' he said sullenly.

They briefly looked over the twisted metal that had previously been an expensive piece of equipment.

'Looks like he got in a wreck,' said Simon.

'He didn't die here though, his luggage has gone. And looking at those tracks I'd say this is where the tractor was that Sarah mentioned.'

Simon discovered a trail of bright crimson blood that was obviously not the thick black mucus of the infected.

It ended where the ruts of heavy tyres began.

'He was injured.'

They followed the gory tracks until they were clear of the innards and meat. As they carried on, the white cab of a vehicle became visible on their left. Beyond that was the farmhouse that was their goal. Within a couple of minutes they realised they were at the right place. Sarah had commented that 'Keep Out' was written in large letters near the roof.

They stood at a collapsed gate looking up the short track past the tractor parked in the middle of the drive a short way ahead.

'This place is dead,' stated Simon.

'Yep no infected around,' nodded Jack.

The door to the tractor was slightly ajar. Jack gripped the grab rails and with his feet on the bottom step pulled himself up to the doorway. There was blood gathered down one side with evidence of emergency triage on the floor. He bent and looked carefully at the bandage wrapper lying there.

'I reckon Randal hit the tractor and got injured. Then he fixed himself up and drove up here looking to hide up for a while.'

'Can you be sure it was him?' asked Simon.

'Not positive, but this blood is no more than a day old, and the bandage wrapper is government marked same as ours,' Jack confirmed.

'That's pretty damning evidence, I reckon. Let's check this house out.'

'Guns.' Jack ordered. They both pulled their pistols from their holsters. They spread apart taking a wide arc towards the door at the side of the house. They checked all around to ensure they wouldn't get jumped from a dark corner of the dilapidated buildings behind them. With no threats present they slowly advanced towards the open heavily damaged door. They pulled the torches from their belts and scanned either side of the door way. Jack entered first and headed towards one side of the dark room as Simon stepped in behind him covering the opposite side. They scanned around the room.

'He was definitely here.' Simon said as he pawed the contents of Randal's damaged pack that was strewn across the large table that took centre stage in the room. A grunt made them both turn their heads towards the doorway that led deeper into the house. Jack being closer to the doorway motioned Simon to hold his position and tiptoed carefully towards it. Thin beams of light criss-crossed the floor from the ill fitted boarded up windows. It appeared to be a sitting room of some type, although one of the armchairs had been repositioned slightly to give a perfect view to the door.

Before he could react the large man was on him. Jack held him back by his shoulders. He was more concerned of the long shard of metal protruding from the man's eye tearing into his face than the gnashing yellow teeth within the bushy grey beard. Jack lost his balance as Simon's body slammed the man away from him. Simon fell aside with the force, the big man kept his feet and Jack was thrown sideways onto the chair which tipped over backwards depositing him on the other side.

The assailant was now attempting to grapple with Simon who was at the disadvantage of being on the floor and wedged against the wall. Jack was on his hands and knees scrabbling about for his discarded pistol. He saw it on the other side of the doorway on the kitchen floor. He cried out in frustration, his pick would take valuable seconds to release from its strapping on his back. Then he saw a brief reflection of gunmetal at his feet.

He picked up the pistol flicked the safety off, aimed roughly and fired. The side of the infected man's head exploded, Simon held against the wall at floor level lifted his legs and kicked the now passive hulk away from him. It landed with a heavy thud like a slab of meat being thrown onto a butcher's chopping block. They held positions for a few seconds breathing heavily the fight now over. Jack tilted the gun he had discovered on the floor. It was Randal's Sig Sauer P226.

The air was thick with cordite as Jack helped Simon up.

'That was a bit close,' breathed Simon.

Jack showed him the Sig 'Randal's still saving our lives,' he said with a smile.

'Now let's get the hell out of here, that gunshot is going to attract them, so we need to get as far away as quick as possible. We've found out what we needed to, our main priority now is to get those girls and their mum back to East 8.

14 RETURN

Since they knew their rough direction back to the house where the girls were situated, they decided to leave the farm to the rear and cut across fields to return. They moved quickly Jack with his pick and Simon with his machete at the ready. One shot from a gun they may have gotten away with, but a second would confirm the Isaiahs of their position.

They dispatched two more slovenly infected on the journey back. Using the hedgerow on the opposite side of the road to the house as cover they moved slowly trying to make as little noise as possible. Through gaps in the greenery they could see a few infected still pawing at the front of the house.

They found a small gap almost opposite the track entrance leading to the rear of the house.

'Shall we just leg it?' said Simon.

'Yeah, they're not gonna get round to the ladder from there till we've long gone up it.'

They edged slowly through the gap one by one until they were standing on the verge in the shade of the overhanging bushes.

'Ready?' said Jack.

'Let's do it.'

Together they bolted across the road, their sudden appearance roused the Isaiahs from their stupor at the house, and they turned and started stumbling in their direction. The men were so much faster than the decaying people, and so sprinted round the back ahead. They could now see the window with the ladder trailing down from it. They veered into the rear garden to be confronted by two undead trying to reach up to the dangling bottom step of the rope ladder. Jack ran harder towards the one on his side, Simon only two paces behind guessed his move. As one they drop kicked their targets into the wall before they'd even registered they were under attack.

Simon had to slash at the head of his with the machete to finish it off. Jack was luckier having slammed its head into the wall so hard it collapsed in a heap on impact. Jack jumped up grabbing the bottom rung and continued to climb hand over hand. He reached the window and clambered in. He turned and leaned out giving Simon a hand to help him through. They looked out to see the first infected from the front appear in the track. After pulling up the ladder they shut the window and sat on the floor with their backs to the wall catching their breath.

Sarah stood in the doorway flanked by the girls.

'How was it?' she asked.

'Our friend is dead. The farmer is as well, his house was wide open. Looks like it's just us five heading back.'

Jack pulled the Sig from his belt and laid it on the floor in front of him.

'You ought to have this. Have you used a gun before?' he queried.

Sarah stepped in and knelt down to pick up the weapon. She deftly dropped the clip out and pulled back the slide to eject the chambered round. She slipped the shell into the top of the clip, flicked the switch so the slide went back to position. She rammed the clip home back into the grip.

'It's safe now.' she smiled. Jack also had a smile, one of admiration. Simon's mouth had dropped open.

'I was a police sergeant before the girls came along.'

They all laughed together for a moment.

'We're going to catch our breath for a few hours, and then Simon will have a look at the car in the neighbour's garage. Hopefully the few that followed us round will have wandered off by then. If not we'll deal with them. If the car is in good shape we'll be leaving the day after tomorrow then.' Jack informed them.

They were ready to head back to East 8. Short of actually starting the car in the garage, Simon was positive it would be fine. Two days earlier at dusk he had silently scaled down the wall and entered through to the garage. The tank was over half full, which was more than enough for their needs. Just in case the fuel was stale he poured a whole bottle of gasoline stabiliser that he always had in his pack for such occurrences. The plugs, oil and water were all fine. It looked like the car was just parked up awaiting its driver until the world disintegrated. The battery tested a little low but he also carried a small jump starter so even that wouldn't be a problem.

'How did you get on?' Jack asked as Simon had clambered back through the window.

'Yeah good. All but started her, should be fine looks well looked after. Even the road tax is still valid.'

'That's a relief, I don't want to be driving illegally.' said Jack with a smile.

Simon and Jack quietly loaded their equipment into the car before dawn. The bikes were now redundant so they left them where they were leaning in the empty garage. Sarah and the girls had very little in the way of possessions due to their hurried escape from the camp they were previously at. Sarah had climbed down but as the girls were a little less able Jack had lowered them one by one, using an improvised rope of sheets, into the waiting arms of both Sarah and Simon.

'Right, we have to do this quickly once the car is started its going to attract every infected in earshot. Don't worry because once we're on the move we'll be fine,' said Jack.

Simon continued 'Jack's driving and I'm riding shotgun, literally. You girls just keep your heads down in the back.'

Having left the passenger door open with everyone else already in the vehicle, Simon went over to the doors at the front of the garage. He silently unlatched them then took his place in the passenger seat and very slowly pulled the door until the lock went click.

'Okay, let's do it.' Jack touched the bare wires and with very little turning over the car started momentarily and died. He looked up at Simon.

'Again,' Simon said quickly.

Jack crossed the wires again. The engine turned and turned. It fired with a cloud of black smoke from behind and died again.

The front door moved as the nearest of the infected were attracted by the new mechanical sound.

'Thank God they haven't the brains to pull the door. Try it again its close now,' Simon said.

A worried sob came from the rear.

'Don't worry girls we'll be out of here in a jiffy.' Jack said as he paired the wires for a third time. The engine turned twice and fired, Jack pushed down on the accelerator and the engine roared.

'Oh yes, thank you German engineering,' Simon said.

Jack twisted the wires together and selected first gear. The car smoothly slid forward, pushing the doors with the front bumper. With a little more gas he moved forward pushing the doors open knocking to the side the Isaiahs that thumped against them. There weren't many others milling around, but their attention was now on the chug chug of the cars motor. They drove away knocking several over as they staggered too close. Once they had left the short driveway and got onto the tarmac Jack was able to accelerate a little more. Sarah looked out the back briefly to see the house they'd been holed up in disappearing into the distance.

The drive back to East 8 was uneventful. Having come along that route only a few days earlier Jack had known where blockages and potential hazards were and diverted accordingly. Having turned off the main road onto the driveway leading to East 8, Simon chose to pick off a few undead with his pistol out of the window. He seldom got any target practise in nowadays. The car was making enough noise so the occasional crack from his own Glock didn't make any difference.

'Seems to be a few more round here than normal.'

Jack nodded in agreement. Occasionally the crews would leave the compound and cull some to keep the numbers down. But more recently they hadn't had to quite as often as fewer had stumbled close enough. They had only turned up in small batches more recently, like the night before they left the haven. It was as if they were grouping together.

The car stopped so suddenly that Simon flinched causing his shot to go wide, ripping into the shoulder of the body next to the one he was aiming at.

'Christ Jack, take it a bit easier mate.'

Jack stared forward and said 'Look!'

The sight that met Simon's eyes ahead stunned him to open mouthed silence. All the fences were either down or compromised, dozens of infected were shambling around inside the compound in varying states of decay. East 8 was far from safe, and there appeared to be no signs of any other survivors. The whole facility was wrecked and as dead as the rest of the country.

15 RESTOCK

'I think we need a change of plan,' said Jack as he turned in his seat to face Simon.

'I'm sure the stores will be worth raiding, and then we need somewhere to go,' he replied.

The car sat idling while they thought fast about their next move.

'We need to get in and out fast, fingers crossed there's very few infected inside.' Jack pointed towards the large gymnasium sitting slightly higher than the surrounding buildings 'Look, the doors are shut to the Ops Room.'

'There might even be survivors inside,' said Sarah from the rear seat.

'You never know! The place seems secure, but I'd have thought they'd have done something to show they were still alive inside,' Simon filled in.

The infected nearby were beginning to converge on where they were parked. Jack began to pull away.

'Ram and plug?' Simon asked him.

'Yep, Ram and plug,' he replied as he built up speed. Simon pulled his seatbelt across him and plugged it in. Jack looked back at Sarah and the girls who were huddled together in the back.

'Put your seatbelts on, it might be a bumpy ride,' he said to them compassionately, then turned back. Simon reloaded their Glock's and placed one in Jack's lap.

The mesh of the already flattened main gate rattled as they sped over it. Jack turned the car sharply and headed for the gymnasium. He lined the car up with the sealed double doors of the entrance. Like a ram raider they hit the doors hard slamming one side open and the other off its hinges flying off to the side of the interior. The car skidded to a halt just inside after scraping both sides on the frame. The engine was still running so Jack rammed it into reverse and pulled backwards to block the hole they had just made.

The inside of the improvised operations room was a complete mess, not only with the detritus of torn maps and broken office equipment, but also bits of ripped apart bodies. Just in front of them laid the tattered remains of a leg and an arm, still partially clothed in what the victims last wore. Sarah gasped at the scene through the windshield. She held the girls tightly and avoided letting them look at the destruction.

The two men got out of the car.

'Stay here Sarah, we really won't be very long,' Jack said 'You've got your gun?'

She nodded.

'Okay, but please hurry,' she replied.

They tentatively picked their way through the debris with guns at the ready. There were more signs of death all over the gymnasium. There were a few figures that didn't belong, a few corpses that had obviously come from outside, their skin was a mottled blue, green, grey. And all had severe head and torso wounds from small arms fire. They moved back together after doing a circuit of the room as the tinkle of spent shell casings could be heard under foot. Jack picked up a disgarded Glock and dropped the clip,

'Empty.' He said placing it on a table.

'It looks like they got it reasonably under control and locked down for a while.' Simon said in hushed tones.

Jack nodded and glanced back towards the car, he could see the dark figures pawing at the back window from the outside. He knew they wouldn't be able to get in and just hoped that Sarah and the girls could cope for another few minutes.

The double doors they now approached were locked, Jack tossed the gun into his left hand and fished around in his inside pocket. He pulled a small key ring out and holding up the longest of the keys smiled at Simon. He slid it into the keyhole and turned it, with a click the door was free. Keeping the keys handy he switched the gun back to his right.

Like a crack military team the two men covered each other as they entered the corridor. In the dull light they could see the corridor had hardly been touched by the violence in the outer room. There were signs of gunplay and some smears of blood close to the door but that was obviously a result of flanking action.

Jack pointed to the door to what had previously been his room a little further up. They worked their way along to it checking all doors and alcoves. Arriving at his own room Jack unlocked the door and went inside leaving Simon as lookout.

The room was as he had left it just a couple of nights before. He grabbed a couple of empty backpacks from his wardrobe and passed one out to Simon. He lifted up a steel box from under the bed. Inside were half a dozen rectangular blocks of plastic explosive, he took a couple. From another compartment in the box he took out some detonators and put them in a pocket. From his drawers he took a couple of boxes of nine millimetre shells and placed them in his pack. He had a final glance around. After replacing the armoured box back underneath the bed he left the room locking the door behind him, habit is a hard thing to shake.

Across the hallway was what had once been a stationary cupboard. Places like this had been utilised as store cupboards all around the complex. Only Shaddock had held the keys for these. Just three kicks and they were in. They stuffed their packs full of MRE's and other basic survival items such as sterilising tablets, torches and some coils of paracord.

'So where are we going to go?' Simon queried.

'There's a place I used to go with the family before all the shit kicked off. The more I think about it the more I like the idea.'

They exited the corridor back into the main room. The car was still waiting where they had left it. They took the most direct route towards it Simon lagging with his full pack.

'Where's that then? Do I know it?'

Just as Jack was about to answer Simon tripped and sprawled onto the filthy, blood drenched floor. He tried to rise just as two hands encrusted with blood grabbed him from underneath the table he was just passing. In panic he slipped entangled with the pack. He tried to pull away from the creature but it would not relinquish its grip on him. As he pulled back the zombie came into view viciously gnashing its teeth, he scrabbled around on the floor and tried to release his pistol from his holster as fingernails clawed at his face and neck.

Tears welled up as he realised the enormity of the injuries he'd just received, he could feel the blood as it trickled down his cheek. Simons hand made contact with his weapon just as the side of the attackers face exploded next to him. He looked up to see Jack standing over him, his Glock held out in front of him smoking. He had a dismayed look on his face.

'I'm sorry Jack,' sobbed Simon 'after all this time.'

'I don't know what to say mate,' said Jack.

'I'll make it easy for you Jack, just go, there must be other groups out there. I've had it Jack; I can feel the darkness invading my head already.' Jack could see the pain etched across his face, his veins already standing out darker than normal. He lifted Simon into a seated position with his back against the table. Blood had soaked down the front of his shirt and was beginning to well up on the floor beneath him.

'Give me some of that C4. I'll buy you some time.'

Jack pulled a block of the explosive from his pack and placed it in Simon's left hand. Jack pulled Simon's Glock from his holster. He dropped the clip out to make sure it had a full magazine. He reinserted it and made the gun ready to fire. He placed it in Simon's rapidly weakening right hand.

'It's been a pleasure to know you Simon.'

'And me to have known you,' he replied with a slur.

'Go Jack! Get those kids out of here.' With that he squeezed Simons hand as a final goodbye gesture. He stood and picked up Simons pack along with his own and headed back towards the car. On reaching it he noticed the girls were still huddled together in the rear, the youngest clutching her cuddly toy tightly, Sarah looked up with a tight lipped smile as Jack jumped into the driver's seat throwing the packs on the passenger seat beside him. He twisted the loose wires together and the car roared back to life. He looked out of the windscreen and smiled at the prone figure of Simon. He looked towards them a weak smile on his face as Jack shifted the car into reverse and gunned the engine. With a jolt the car sped backwards knocking through the horde leaving streaks of foul effluent along the car windows and dented bodywork. As the mob cleared he swung the car round sharply causing a couple to sprawl across the bonnet. He shifted into first gear and the car bounced over the detritus strewn around. Putting his foot down he sideswiped many of the infected, some being drawn under the wheels and some being catapulted like ragdolls away from the car knocking others down like bowling pins. They joined the road and headed away from the now compromised East 8.

He looked in his mirror and could see that the majority of the infected were flooding through the hole left by the car and into the gym. He saw the flash before the thunder of the explosion reached them. For a moment he thought about Simon and his sacrifice then he was interrupted by Sarah.

'Where do we go now?'

'I have an idea, somewhere I know. Do you like the seaside girls?' he said with a smile.

16 INPENETRABLE

For a while they travelled in silence, just the chugging of the car and the breeze from the open windows breaking it.

'Where's the funny man?' said Sally.

Before Sarah got to answer, Jack beat her to concocting a reply.

'He wanted to stay and tidy up. He said to say goodbye to you both though.'

Sarah forced a smile and catching Jacks eye's in the rear view mirror mouthed a 'thank you'. The further they got away from East 8 the fewer infected were around. They cut off the main roads and took small lanes and tracks which decreased them even more.

Jack took several turns and before long they had come across a public house. He pulled the car up outside on the main road.

'Let's see if we have any company,' he said as he retrieved his pistol from the passenger seat. He wound down the window stuck out his arm and fired once.

'What was that in aid of?' Sarah asked.

'Just want to see if there are any infected about. And here they come.'

Two walking corpses both struggled to get out of the open pub entrance at the same time. One was a heavy set man, the other a virtually naked woman with rags hanging from her shoulders, the distinctive mottled grey skin colour of the dead.

Jack got out of the car and strode over to them ice pick in his hand. Sarah attracted the girls' attention out to the opposite side of the car.

He kicked the woman to the ground as he swung the pick and embedded it in the large man's head. He quickly retrieved it and before the girl had got to her feet he swung it again into her face. Within two seconds both were dealt with. He walked into the musty smelling bar room. His ruse had worked and the bar was clear of infected. As he suspected any food and drink up front had already been ransacked many times over, apart from the odd missed item.

He headed behind the bar, broken glass carpeted the floor. He kicked around on the floor and tipped the corner of the rug up. With a little more kicking the rug was moved clear and the hatch to the cellar was exposed.

He knelt and felt around for the recessed hoop that would allow him to lift the trap door. On finding it he pulled the door up and threw it aside leaving the dark cavern unprotected. He delved his hand into his thigh pocket and retrieved a small pencil type torch and shone it into the cellar. Dust motes danced in the beam, but apart from that there was nothing untoward. He climbed down the steps and looked around, the inoperable pumps still had barrels attached, the contents of which by now would have gone off. The sealed barrels would have fared better. Then the light caught the bottles of clear liquid he had been looking for. Six cases of mineral water were stacked on a low shelf.

After passing them up to the ground floor he then transferred them onto the bar. Sarah stood half in and half out the door,

'Is everything okay?' she asked.

'Good timing, you can help me carry these back to the car. Is it still clear outside?'

'Yes fine, so where are you taking us?'

Jack gave her a case of water to go under each arm. Then he picked up the last four cases himself.

'It's the perfect place on the coast,' Jack said as he followed her out of the door.

Just over an hour later they pulled the battered car into a sandy cliff top car park. They had fuel to spare but the car had not retained a single straight panel and the engine was misfiring towards the end of their journey.

They left the car secured at the top of the car park. Jack led Sarah and the girls to the long stairway that sloped down the cliff towards the sea. Jack opened the gate and took the lead. Sarah tightly gripped her daughters' hands for their descent down the endless looking staircase carved out of the bedrock.

After a couple of minutes the red and white lighthouse came into view, it was perched solidly on a rocky outcrop with just an outbuilding attached, as they got closer a boathouse with slipway appeared further down the cliff.

Cautiously Jack checked out all the buildings, as Sarah apprehensively waited outside with her children. It wasn't long before he reappeared at the reinforced lighthouse door.

'All clear in there,' he shouted to Sarah 'just going to check the boathouse.'

With that she and the girls entered their new found fortress. With a smile she thought to herself that maybe things were on the change.

Jack stood by as the three entered their new home. He gently pushed the door shut behind them to the sounds of the girls utterances of joy and wonder.

He smiled as he wandered down to check out the boathouse. The weathered door was unlocked; he opened it tentatively clutching the gun in case of trouble. As he stepped inside the recognisable smell of human decay hit him in the face. Jack stayed close to the wall pistol at the ready.

As his eyes became accustomed to the gloom he moved slowly around the footway. Then a guttural moan grew close by. He immediately saw the infected man's arms thrashing. Jack chortled when he realised the infected sailor was severely tangled up within some rigging hanging from the wall. He approached the subdued man and leisurely placed his gun back in its holster, and removed the ice pick. He despatched the man with ease and disposed of his body down the slipway and into the sea before returning to Sarah and the girls.

From what they'd seen most of the undead were headed away from the coast and inland where the bigger conurbations were. This lighthouse was two miles from the nearest main road, fifteen from the nearest town, and even if they did get out this far they then had the solid gate and a few hundred yards of staircase to contend with, which was the only access to the lighthouse and its associated outbuildings.

The advantages were many, unfortunately so were the disadvantages. On a plus note, they were very remote and inaccessible. The lighthouse itself was impregnable, but the biggest advantage was that they had power, at one time the lighthouse had been manned using gas powered lights but in recent years it had been upgraded and reborn as an unmanned drone.

As such it benefitted from solar panel rechargeable battery power circuits, not only that but the original propane generators were still in place as a second option complete with a massive propane tank in one of the outbuildings. And just to top it off there was a washing machine.

On the minus side the ground was so rocky and infertile self-sufficiency would be impossible, regular scavenging hunts would be required. Jack had an ingenious plan with regard to fresh vegetables. There were houses within four miles of their present position, and close by were some overgrown allotments. However they would have been overgrown with self-seeded vegetables, just because human life had ceased to be the main inhabitant plants were growing unchecked. Jacks plan was that once they had settled he would enclose the entire allotment with fencing, then visit on occasion by bicycle and retrain the entire area giving them an offsite farm.

They had scavenged other items on the way to their new home. A small catalogue store they found in a market town turned out to be a goldmine. They had two backpacks stuffed full of emergency rations from East 8, water from the pub and bedding from the store.

For the first time in a long time Jack slept properly all night, albeit on a camp bed in the lamp room.

17 COMFORT

The following days after their arrival at the lighthouse they got to work making the area more secure and the rooms a little more comfortable. Jack went out and procured a more solid gate which he concreted into the ground at the car-park end of the staircase. He also made a foray back to the catalogue store where they got the bedding from and managed, with the help of an abandoned builder's flatbed truck, to return with a couple of buildable beds and some other pieces of useful flat-pack furniture. He also couldn't resist a dusty display of various toys in the foyer which he knew the girls would appreciate.

Charlotte and Sally were now starting to lose their feral look, from the shock of what they had witnessed and were becoming more sociable by the day. Charlotte was still a little more reserved than her younger sister. He hoped the toys he returned with would help bring her out of her shell a little more.

Jack missed his two friends as if they were lost family members. To compensate he was almost putting his all into protecting the three girls, although Sarah was now getting back her independence having lost the sheep mentality of pretty much being a prisoner at the refugee camp.

The lighthouse consisted of a ground-floor which had a line of kitchen units, a gas cooker and a fridge freezer, which was the dubious task of Jack to clean out. The kitchen area took up a third of the curved wall. The entire floor became their kitchen, diner and lounge. The second floor was used as a communal bedroom, Sarah and her daughters shared a king-size bed. They even had a toilet, of sorts; it was basically a hatch that released the effluent down the cliff edge.

Above the second level sat the lamp room. Jack took this over as his space, doubling as bedroom and lookout tower. He was welcome to share the second floor with the others but had declined saying 'it was their space'. In reality what he actually wanted was his space. With the crew it was a partnership, with these survivors he felt that his job was looking after them. He was slightly uncomfortable with the reason why he felt he had to be their protector when so many others had been left aside since the crisis had begun. He just couldn't put his finger on why he felt that way.

In the lamp room a camp bed was set up and Jack spent most of his rest time sat on a chair gazing back inland and occasionally out to sea.

He was becoming worried about the situation with the walking corpses, he seldom saw the undead nowadays, but when he did they were no longer in ones and twos, they were now generally large groups of twenty plus. He thought that they should have pretty much disintegrated by now, after all to all intent and purpose they were dead and surely the decomposition process should have ended months ago.

He felt that they were flocking together which could be a serious problem if they got into larger hordes. Up to ten are easy to control and put down, but upwards of that all you can do is run. Even fences and walls could easily tumble with the pressure of thousands against it. A mere seedling has the strength to push through the earth and even tarmac, as nearly all roads displayed now through lack of use.

It was early; even the sun wasn't yet above the horizon. The sea air was revitalising as Jack left the lighthouse. As he closed the door Sarah on the other side locked it and went back to the warmth of the bed, the girls not yet awake. He slung the pack and rifle over his shoulder and started the ascent of the long staircase. It was sizing up to be a bright and clear day, the sea was calm. Resting part way up taking the rifle scope from his belt he scanned all round, as usual there was nothing but the detritus floating around near the shore. Rubbish from across the seas and the occasional inert body being gently caressed by the ebb and flow of the tide.

He spun around to view the gate at the end of the staircase ahead. He paused and held his breath. The area outside the gate was heaving with the undead; it was as if they could sense the living beyond. There were not quite enough to flatten the fence, but he knew more could be attracted. He decided that there was nothing mysterious about their appearance. He had been coming and going a lot recently, with scavenging the local area and his gardening efforts at the allotments a few miles away. The sound of his engines in the predominantly silent land must have attracted them from miles around.

He hung his pack on the safety fence that ran along both sides of the stairs. He then scaled it and after retrieving his bag proceeded in climbing to sit atop a large boulder. Once comfortable he had an excellent view of the gate that was still a hundred yards or so away. He didn't need to see the rotting corpses as the gentle breeze wafted their fowl stench towards him in little blasts.

Taking a box of rifle shells from his pack he placed them close to hand on the rock. After he fitted the scope to his ex-police sniper rifle, he unclipped its bipod and lay prone but comfortable behind it. He took careful aim at his first mark. The scope was powerful and he could even make out the maggots falling from its ear. It was horribly desiccated with leather-like skin stretched taught across its bones. Jack levelled the crosshairs of the scope on the centre of its face. He breathed slowly and gently squeezed the trigger.

The recoil was heavily suppressed by a spring loaded stock, the crack was sharp but actually not as loud as he remembered. The suppressor seemed to do a good job. The bullet entered just above the cadaver's right eye, a small hole appeared a millisecond after the report, and a waft of dust drifted in almost a spurt from the rear of its head. It slowly dropped down under the throng.

Time and time again his shots hit the mark. As he singled out each zombie and despatched them, he thought about the whole situation on a global and local scale. He was calm and calculated, the safe position and the fact he had more than enough ammunition to deal with this lot made him feel as if he really was master of the new safe haven they had created.

The camp Sarah and the girls were at had been attacked by a large horde, East 8 assumingly also fallen to a horde, although the state of the fences could have been a factor. And now it seemed that this stronghold was also under threat, not right now but a horde twice the size of this would breach the gate without too much effort. If he didn't know better he'd think the human race was being systematically destroyed. Maybe they had attacked the largest groups of survivors first then intended mopping up the smaller bands. But his paranoia was causing the daydream, when you think about an untenable situation most people generally think of the worst case scenario.

As the final cadaver fell he finally looked up from the steaming rifle to view the mound of corpses lying by the gate. On counting up his used shells he made it seventy eight and it had taken a good couple of hours to deplete them as the sun was much higher in the sky.

After the smoke had cleared he went up to the carpark and dealt with the dead. With the aid of some foundry gloves he dragged and carried all the bodies to the entrance of the car park and piled them close to the road. Before heading back to the lighthouse, he took a can of petrol from one of his stockpiled vehicles and dowsed the heap. With the aid of a match he lit some ragged clothing of an accessible corpse, and the pyre caught very quickly. He stood back as the flames grew. He thought hard, he needed information they couldn't be all that's left of the human race. There was only one place he knew where he might get a few more answers.

18 FRUSTRATION

Jack sat quietly in his chair at the top of the lighthouse in the lens room; he was leaning back looking into the distance. He watched in contemplation as the smoke from the pyre silently billowed up in the darkening evening sky. He had been so wrapped up in his own thoughts that he failed to hear the footsteps coming up the spiral staircase on the opposite side of the inoperable lamp, something he had disconnected early on their arrival to conserve power.

'A penny for your thoughts?'

Startled he looked around to find Sarah standing at the top of the metal staircase holding two steaming mugs.

'Oh, I was just thinking about the next step,' he replied with a smile. 'How are the girls?'

'They're sound asleep. They seem to sleep so much better now.'

She headed around the circular walkway past the lamp and handed him one of the mugs before taking a seat on a folding chair beside him.

'I hope you don't mind me saying, but I fail to see that there is a next step. We're safe here, aren't we?'

'But for how long?' he replied 'Haven't you noticed we rarely see lone Isaiah's nowadays? They all seem to be in larger groups. If a passing horde is big enough they will get in.'

'Maybe they're like buses wait around for ages and three turn up all at once.' She said in an effort to lighten the conversation.

'I really am concerned Sarah,' he said more seriously, 'I think they're massing together like locusts. If only a handful turn up at the gate I can handle them like this morning, but if a massive horde turns up this lighthouse will become our tomb. I'm thinking about some sort of escape plan among other things.'

Sarah moved her hand onto his leg and squeezed his knee gently.

'If it wasn't for you we'd be out there trying to get at you right now, either that or we'd be three of the smouldering corpses in the car park.'

Looking into his eyes Sarah leant forward. Jack hadn't been kissed by a woman for some time. Love was a forgotten concept. It was ironic that man was beginning to become extinct and the last thing on his mind was to procreate. Her lips gently caressed his and he reciprocated.

Gently he pushed her away.

'You owe me nothing,' he said 'Life is far more precious now than it used to be.'

'I owe you my life and that of my children, and I'm kissing you because I want to.' With that she passionately caressed him again.

'Look Sarah;' he said pushing her back for a second time 'I need to find out more, we can't be all that's left, and I've decided I need to go back to East 8 to see what I can find out.'

She suddenly stood and pleaded 'You don't have to. Let's just enjoy the rest while we can. I can't see that you'll find out anything from there anyway?'

'Having been a partial government venture there must be information available. Up till a few months ago we were still getting supply drops by helicopter. We never questioned it, never needed to. Everybody had their jobs and dealing with incoming supplies wasn't ours. My assumption was that there must've been a bigger network, after all we never had a chopper, so they must've been slightly better organised than us.'

Sarah sat and contemplated for a moment 'You said they stopped delivering a few months ago, to me it sounds like they're probably gone too.'

'I need to be sure Sarah, if there's a chance of better survival for all of us and a plan to fight back, I want to be part of it.'

'Ah, now we get down to the crux of it, you want revenge.'

'Of course, I want revenge! Those bloody things took everything I cared about away. I want them all dead and this time so they won't get up.'

'You've got us here, we care about you.' Sarah said angrily motioning her arm at the staircase implying the children would agree.

Jack calmed himself down, 'I know and I'm sorry. I've thought hard about this, the girls can't stay shut away in here for the rest of their lives. If there's a chance of better survival out there with maybe some sort of stable community I need to know.'

'You've always got to be doing something,' Sarah said as she sipped her coffee. 'Were you like that before all this mess?'

'You're probably right, yes. There never was enough time, but then I was doing it to get more for my family, now I have to keep busy to stay alive.'

His lips were held tight as he reminisced back to his old life and a time when he didn't need to check his back constantly, just the bank balance and making sure the bills for things that no longer existed were paid. Rent, mortgage, hire purchase, credit cards and money no longer had value. A tin of baked beans, a bottle of water, a blade and a gun were now the only currency. The person with an armoury was a rich man.

'We didn't know how lucky we were back then.' Sarah agreed.

She placed the mug on the floor beside her chair and leant towards him. Jack turned his head so that their faces were a mere couple of inches apart. They gazed into each other's eyes for what seemed like an eternity.

He could not take the longing for Sarah anymore he moved forward and their lips met again. They gently parted as the two passionately kissed. The trials and tribulations of what was going on outside the lamp room was momentarily forgotten.

They intertwined their arms around each other, hugging tightly as if trying to morph into one. They eased apart as Sarah pulled away slowly standing. She drew her fingers down his arm until she reached his hand and gripped it.

He looked up at her in the moonlight as she moved past him heading towards his bed space on the floor. Her silhouette was perfectly formed. Her leggings and tee shirt accentuated her figure increasing his desire for her.

As he rose at her silent insistence he could feel the tightness in his loins. Something he never thought he would ever feel again. She sat down on the edge of his thin mattress, and pulled her arms through the arms of her tee shirt pulling it off and over her head. Jack pulled off his own shirt and knelt down to her beckoning arms. For a short while all was forgotten in a wave of pure ecstasy.

The sun had long since dropped below the horizon and darkness had blocked much of the view of the land. Moonlight was beginning to glint off the sea highlighting the white tips of the breaking waves. The only light was the warm glow of the candles from the floor below emanating up the staircase.

They lay together naked in the darkness.

'I better get back down and turn in,' Sarah whispered as she leaned over him gathering her clothing together.

'Of course, .'

Sarah kissed his cheek and rose from the bed, she collected the two mugs. One hand on the top of the stair rail she looked back. In the warm glow of the candle light from below, he saw her smile.

'Goodnight, my hero.' She said suppressing a giggle.

'And to you.' He replied as she continued her descent to the second floor.

She stood and looked at the sleeping forms in the king-size bed, they looked peaceful, Charlotte sucking her thumb and Sally snuggled up to her toy, Pyewacket. She blew out one of the two candles and carried on down to the ground floor. She placed the empty mugs in the sink, placed her hands on its edge and dropped her head forwards. Over the short time she had known Jack she had become used to having him around and didn't want him to leave. But she understood his reasons for going back. When it came down to it he wanted what was best for them all, a new life not just an existence.

She checked the heavy bolts were drawn on the steel entrance door and headed back up to the bedroom.

The candlelight disappeared suddenly from the stairwell and Jack was bathed in utter darkness.

He went back to sitting on the chair gazing out of the curved full height window. His eyes had become a little more accustomed to the darkness. His decision was already made despite what they had just shared. What they had just done was something they both needed, love wasn't an option as there was so much left to do, not yet anyway, maybe in the future if there was going to be one. He still loved his family whatever and wherever they were now, and nothing and no one would ever stop that.

19 SEA

The next morning Jack was up at the crack of dawn. He quietly headed down to the ground floor so as not to disturb the still sleeping girls. He took his Glock from the cupboard and grabbed a bottle of water from another. The bolts slid open on the door with a metallic scrape. He pushed open the door and stepped outside; it was cool but again clear. Since hell had appeared on earth, the weather seemed to have become milder which was probably due to the lack of pollution from the end of manufacturing Worldwide.

He walked along a pathway that headed past the generator building attached to the lighthouse and down to the boathouse. The treads had been cut into the rock of the cliffs decades before, an age highlighted by the well weathered building it led towards.

Before he returned back to East 8 he wanted to be sure all angles were covered for Sarah and the girls. He had already raided every house and shop in the vicinity. Despite there being very few he had managed to scavenge enough supplies to last a few months.

In the boathouse sat a hard bottomed marine dinghy, not a speed boat but still a good sturdy vessel. There were even a range of four outboard motors to choose from. Jack went to work getting one of the engines fit for work. Being a practical man he could usually turn his hand to anything. He knew very little about outboards but one thing he did know eliminated the first three he looked at. The last one, the bulkiest and not the prettiest was diesel powered. Especially as there was a well-stocked diesel tank in the generator room, and diesel doesn't go off.

After three hours of tinkering Jack was ready to test drive the boat. He hadn't run the engine yet as the prop head needed to be underwater to aid cooling. The boat house was a dry one.

He opened up the double doors allowing a cool ocean breeze to invade the still air of the workshop. The slope of the slipway stretched steadily down into the beige froth-lined breaking waves. He stepped back along the gangway; he paused briefly to ensure he had secured the motor properly on the tail board then continued on towards the cranking mechanism which would lower the silver dinghy into the water.

The door into the building opened as he began to wind the crank handle and Sarah accompanied by her daughters entered.

He stopped momentarily and greeted them.

'Hey guys, how is everybody?'

'Just wanted to let you know I'm just doing some lunch,' said Sarah.

'Me and Pyewacket stirred the gravy,' piped up Sally holding out her stuffed cat.

Jack bent to Sally's level

'Very well done you two,' he said and dabbed an oily finger print on her nose, she giggled wiping furiously.

'And what about you Charlotte? Want a dab.' The older girl grinned and slid to hide behind her mother.

'Keep those filthy mitts away from me mister,' Sarah laughed backing off. 'How are you getting on anyway?'

'Funny you should ask. I was just about to try her out. Do you want to come?'

'Let's eat first, then we could all go out,' Sarah replied. 'Fancy going for a boat ride girls?' Both nodded in reply to their mother.

'That's settled then. After lunch we'll go out for a boat-trip,' Jack agreed.

The ocean cruise was enlightening. It was as if they were television viewers watching disaster unfold from the comfort of their own living rooms. In the boat they travelled around five miles along the coast after a quick few circles close to the boathouse to ensure the outboard was fine. They saw a great deal of dereliction. A couple of small villages in ruins and a resort that appeared to have been burnt to the ground, the only remaining undamaged item being a smoke darkened sign that read 'Enjoy the beachfront' which sported a giant smiling cartoon face wearing a sombrero.

At one point they travelled within fifty feet of a pier. Up until that point they hadn't seen any of the infected other than the occasional floating corpse. More often than not they were totally inanimate, live ones tended to fill quickly with water and sink to the depths below. Jack had to deal with one flailing corpse wearing a lifejacket that floated a little close for comfort; Sarah ensured the girls looked away as Jack shot the creature in the head.

The pier was seemingly teeming with death. The majority followed the sound of the outboard, their instinct leading them. Jack witnessed several hundred step from the end of the pier and disappear into the waves below as they passed.

Jack steered the boat away from the pier and headed back towards their lighthouse. Thankfully the girls were becoming immune to the destruction before them. Youth was resilient. It was a situation where if your mind didn't come to terms, with desolation and survival becoming the norm, insanity would take over.

When they finally got back to the boat house it was almost dusk. Jack slowly drove the boat onto the slip where he stepped out. With the aid of a rope he pulled the craft to position it on the dolly. Sarah and the girls stayed put as Jack wound the crank drawing the boat back inside. Jack helped the girls disembark. He took Sarah's hand,

'If you had to, would you be okay to launch and pilot this boat?' he said quietly.

'Oh I see,' she said. 'You're going back aren't you?'

'I am. Even if I find nothing out, there's still practical stuff we can use.'

'Doesn't matter what I say or do you're still going.'

'I'm afraid so, I have a friend I need to lay to rest there.'

Sarah nodded solemnly.

'Right girls.' she said loudly following and catching up with the girls further along the pathway

'Cocoa, then bed.'

Jack held back letting them get ahead. He wanted to keep a mental image of the backdrop of the magnificent lighthouse, with the two pretty girls and a beautiful woman heading towards it. To him it felt like a day trip with the dead world a million miles away. He promised himself he would return.

The following morning Jack was up early, before light. Even if he found nothing out at East 8 at least he might be able to replenish certain supplies like pistol and rifle ammunition of which they had plenty, but you never could have too much. The meals in ready to eat ration packs were also getting low, not overly essential as they had every tin of food from miles around anyway. It was always handy to have some in case of emergency. Fresh vegetables were becoming scarcer but come spring more than they could handle would be available in the plots he'd tended and retrained.

Sarah had become a much stronger person while they'd been at the lighthouse. It's like she'd had time to take a breather and assess her own situation the shock of the speed in which the world collapsed had left her reeling, left them all in some kind of shock. Sarah and the girls had been treated like cattle in the hastily prepared military run camp they'd been at. It had been pure luck together with her survival instinct and resilience that they had got away at all. He could see she was strong enough to look after her girls if anything was to happen to him.

He fished around in the bowl of tagged keys which resided on the kitchen worktop. Finding the ones labelled Range Rover he placed them in the pocket of his combats. Before leaving the building he paused and decided that he would say goodbye after all. He climbed the stairs to the next level and approached the bed. With a gentle smile he gazed at the faces of the sleeping girls and then met eyes with Sarah. Looking sad she forced a smile.

'You're not coming back are you?' she whispered.

'If there's one thing I'm sure of, if it's at all possible, I'm coming back for you.'

Bending over he kissed her warm lips.

The previous evening had been very pleasant. A few board games where Jack made sure he lost to Charlotte and Sally, so he had told Sarah. But she wasn't so sure they hadn't beaten him properly. After the girls turned in, Jack and Sarah talked about the old world, favourite music, preferred movies and television programmes.

Then afterwards he sat looking out to sea, at one point he thought he glimpsed a light way out on the horizon, but on a clear night such as this staring out across the expanse often played tricks on his eyes.

It was the second hardest thing he had ever done, leaving these three girls and the relative safety of the lighthouse. If he didn't go though, how much longer would it be safe and how long before it became their tomb?

The walk up the steps in the cool morning drizzle was peaceful, his mind thinking of Sarah and the forgotten feelings he was beginning to feel for her. But now as he reached the gate his mind was on the job in hand. The car park was littered with an assortment of vehicles that they had amassed over the time they'd been there. He walked past the car they escaped from the house and East 8 in, and the builder's flatbed to the almost pristine Range Rover. He loaded his pack onto the passenger seat as he climbed in. The powerful turbo diesel motor roared to life as he turned the key in the ignition.

As he drove out towards the road he stopped adjacent to the pile of ash and bones and looked back towards the lighthouse. He smiled then gunned the automatic engine and pulled out onto the tarmac heading back to East 8.

20 ANSWERS

By mid-morning he pulled up to the flattened gate to East 8. The road had been kind, all the diversions were clear and everything was pretty much the same as when they had previously travelled that way, apart from one thing. He saw just one walker on this journey. On their initial drive to the coast they had seen quite a few, but now it seemed they had all disappeared. Most probably drawn to a sound or an event of some kind he supposed.

East 8 was still wrecked with even less life than the previous visit. There weren't even any walkers in the vicinity. The gymnasium was pretty much four blackened walls, it looked like the fire caused by the explosion burnt unchecked for some time, as there were still wisps of smoke or steam rising from the rubble.

Slowly driving over the flattened fence he headed for the hall, it was quiet and foreboding in the dull daylight, it resembled old Abbey ruins, as opposed to a modern sports hall cum operations centre for the whole of the post disaster eastern region.

He pulled up short of the gaping hole that had been the double doors they'd bashed through weeks before. The utility belt was fastened and he holstered his sidearm and trusty pick axe, although it seemed totally deserted he wasn't taking any chances. Jack left the car and headed cautiously into the ominous looking building. He kept a good look out for any possibility of collapse as well as the infected, the last thing he needed was to be struck by falling masonry then eaten alive unable to move.

The centre of the room was blasted clear with a small indented crater caused by the C4 Simon had ignited to aid their escape. There was no sign of the Simon's body, but there were plenty of blackened bones sticking out of the rumble towards the edges of what was left of the gym. He felt a little remorse at not being able to put his friend to rest.

There were also plenty of rats and mice skulking about in the shadows, they were certainly thriving with the current situation and the abundance of carrion. The smell of rotten meat was evident around the edges where, he assumed, the vermin had made they nests. With torch in hand he headed over to the corridor, now door less, where the general quarters were situated. It seems the fire hadn't spread too far towards the other blocks despite what he initially thought. Smoke damage was less severe, the burnt bacon smell hung nearly as heavily but not as sickening as the putrid flesh. He passed his old room, it was still locked. There was nothing he needed from it this time so he passed by continuing towards the dining room and his goal, Shaddock's quarters. If anyone knew of the situation it would have been him.

Jack wondered what had happened to him, maybe he bugged out? He would think Shaddock would have held out, if anyone was a born survivor it would've been him.

Going deeper into the building the damage became less and less, although the burnt smell was ever present. The door to Shaddock's private rooms was closed but thankfully not locked, the silence was unnerving and Jack felt that to break it with smashing a door down could be a mistake, the building was far from secure and there were dark corners everywhere, and he was a little on edge as it was.

The room was virtually untouched, quite a large room with an en-suite. The single bed was neatly made complete with hospital corners. Jack giggled, somehow that didn't surprise him having known Shaddock. He liked to cross the T's and dot the i's. On the opposite wall was a desk with a couple of filing cabinets either side.

He closed the door behind him. The bathroom was an unknown entity. He gently placed his ear against the frosted glass and listened for any sound that would suggest someone incumbent.

To his surprise the door suddenly opened inwards forcing him to fall briefly sideways. His head came to rest on the cold steel barrel of a revolver. The gun was pushed into his temple forcing him upright. He turned slightly to look into the unshaven face of Shaddock. Immediately the gun was lowered.

'Jack, oh my lord am I happy to see a friendly face.'

'Shaddock? I assumed everybody either died or bugged out.'

Shaddock took on a stern expression 'Nobody got away.' He pulled up his sleeve to reveal a dark blood encrusted bandage wrapped around his lower arm.

'I was scavenging a couple of days ago and I was caught by one of them, it was half buried under the rubble.'

'That's bad news.' Said Jack genuinely disappointed 'What the hell happened?'

'To put it bluntly, Jack, you were right.' Shaddock limped past him and took a seat on the neatly made bed and motioned Jack to take his office chair opposite. Jack turned and dropped the latch on the door before sitting down.

'In the early hours of the morning, the day after you left, a large horde of infected hit the fences on the east, it collapsed almost immediately. I should have taken notice of your concerns.' Shaddock continued, 'They were inside the complex before the alarm was raised. Most survivors didn't stand a chance. We managed to push them back to the gym, a dozen of us, and eventually managed to hold them off long enough to lock the doors.'

'What happened to the rest?' Jack eyed him suspiciously.

'To be honest, we weren't very thorough, most already had been infected. Two took their own lives,' Shaddock took a breath 'I was close to doing the same before you turned up. Hope has kept me going.'

'Hope for what? If everyone else is dead what were you waiting to happen?'

'Rescue of course, not everyone was privy to that information, but now it doesn't really matter as I'm going no-where. There is a safe zone.'

'I thought there might be its why I've come back. I knew if one existed the information about it would be here.' Jack said.

'Oh yes my dear boy, that and more. Everything anyone knows about this whole situation is in my desk. There are even some things that they don't know in the secure area, which by the way, is the whole of Scotland.'

Jack was momentarily stunned, 'The whole of Scotland?' he repeated.

'That's right, Hadrian's Wall had been hastily re-fortified and there's a few million people living merrily on the other side. That's where the choppers were coming from, well they relayed here via gas rigs in the North Sea.'

'But the drops stopped six months ago,' said Jack.

'They were suspended, apparently the barrier to the safe zone was hit by a massive horde numbering in the thousands. It caused a great deal of death and destruction. As a result all hands were needed on deck, so to speak. We were told on the last drop.'

'So there is a chance we can take the country back?' queried Jack.

'If there is, that will be the place to find out,' replied Shaddock. 'I'm not feeling very well Jack, I think I need to have a nap. I know time is running out for me, so please help yourself to my files you'll know as much as I if you go through them.'

'That's good of you, I have survivors with me, children, I want to get them to safety,' said Jack.

Shaddock sat up on the bed and proceeded to make himself comfortable by bulking up the pillows. He looked Jack in the eye 'Jack, I'm going to go to sleep. Now let me make this clear to you. I do not want to wake up,' he said clearly. 'Do you understand what I'm saying?'

Jack understood he smiled and said 'Thanks for everything Shaddock, now settle down and get some sleep. Goodnight.'

'No Jack, thank you for coming back, at last I'll be able to rest. Good luck my friend.' He closed his eyes and fitfully drifted off to sleep.

Jack decided to give Shaddock a couple of hours sleep before putting him out of his misery. He felt more comfortable having another person present while he worked his way through the information at hand, despite that person being asleep.

He found a pad and proceeded to make notes from the various files and paperwork on the desk in front of him. One particular file caught his eye. Within the stack was a folder containing information regarding all the staff at East 8. They appeared to know a great deal about everyone. Jack was intrigued to know what they thought about him.

After locating the entry about himself he read on. His life was documented parents, schools, wife and children. All the information was concise but correct and incredibly well researched. The final remarks at the end surprised him,

'Jack has a great talent that was wasted in his pre-disaster career. His hate for the undead is only matched by his hate for authority. But he has proved to be invaluable in the running of this facility and one person I would trust with control in the event of expansion. He would make an excellent area commander when control has been retaken.'

Jack turned his chair and looked back to the sleeping form of Shaddock. He knew what he had to do, and he needed to deal with him before he passed out with tiredness himself. The idea of sleeping in a room with someone who would probably change within a couple of hours was something Jack couldn't even contemplate.

He took a few important documents and his notes and placed them inside a pocket folder. The knowledge he had just acquired was far more than he had imagined. His next move would be to deal with Shaddock then after some rest head back to the lighthouse.

In one of the drawers Jack had discovered a small .22 calibre pistol. He turned down the barrel to display the four chambers filled with small cartridges. It was perfect for the job required.

Jack stood over Shaddock, he was almost gone, his skin was pale and almost translucent in the dull glow being emitted by the lamp on the desk. His sleep was fitful and sweat almost poured from him. Jack gently pulled out one of his pillows. He gently placed over the sleeping form and pressed the small pistol into it. He held his breath and closed his eyes as he pulled the small trigger. The crack it emitted surprised him with its loudness despite being dulled by the improvised silencer. He removed the pillow and saw the small hole just below Shaddock's temple. Shaddock had been put to rest and was now at peace.

    Jack gathered up his equipment and the all-important folder. He unlocked the door and keeping the lamp low he headed back down the corridor towards his own old room, torch guiding his way through the darkness. It was as he'd left it. He locked himself in and lay down on the bed to sleep. The aroma of the fire was still in the air but he did not care. Exhaustion had finally got the better of him and he was out like a light.

21 HOMEWARD

Jack awoke next morning with a start. There was sound. Not loud but subtle noises of shuffling and an overwhelming monotone drone in the air. The dizziness of awakening suddenly subsided quickly as he got his bearings. He understood what was happening straight away and suspected the building had been surrounded by infected whilst he had slept.

Locked in his room he felt safe but hemmed in. He had food but no water, and he was thirsty. He had to get out, a couple of hours at the most otherwise dehydration would affect his judgement and strength.

He rifled through the drawers in his desk. The second one he tried revealed what he was looking for. He tore the small cardboard box in two to reveal the pill packet. He popped two out into his palm and threw them into his mouth swallowing them dry. The caffeine tablets should give him a little more energy to aide his escape.

He folded the all-important file and pushed it securely down the back of his trousers. With a tightening of his belt and clothing he checked his Glock and ensured he had a few more clips in his combat trousers. Looking through the single frosted window in his door he tried to get an idea of numbers in the corridor, but it was too dark. Slowly he unlocked the door and pushed it open a few inches. There were figures outside shuffling aimlessly along the corridor. He eased the door shut again. He breathed heavily tightly gripping the pick.

Jack pushed open the door hard. Two infected close by were knocked off their feet, several more along the corridor turned at the commotion. Adrenaline and caffeine kicked in and he rushed towards ops. He knocked aside all the infected in his way with his shoulder, choosing to make ground and not waste time braining them.

On reaching the derelict operations room he took a breather. There were few inside but he could see the majority of the pack passing by the holes and more importantly the exit to the car parked beyond. It seemed like an endless torrent shambling past. The horde was monstrous and continued to pass by, all heading in the same direction. He had no choice, to go back to the safety of his room now would be suicide he had to just plough through and pray he would make it to the car.

Using the rubble as cover Jack moved closer to the exit, the undead still stumbled past. A noise distracted him from behind; he turned to see three what only could be described as rotting corpses bearing down on him, hitting the first around the head with the blunt side of the pick knocked it off kilter, while it spun he plunged the pick into the seconds face. The third hit him dead centre knocking him to the ground, he felt pain from the rubble beneath him as he grappled to get the upper hand.

Red mist hit and another adrenaline burst pushed him harder. With a free hand he grabbed at the debris hoping to get hold of anything he could use. Picking something long up he jabbed it into the attacking zombie's mouth causing it to gag fowl smelling fluid, he shoved and pushed until the blackened thigh bone he had attacked with exited through the back of the corpses head.

Jack winched as a searing pain struck like lightning through the side of his head.

He pushed the body that he'd just slaughtered with the bone off himself, and pulled away from the first one he'd previously stunned. Looking into its face he could see the crimson dripping from its chin and the broken teeth chewing on part of his ear, fuelled by pure hatred he jumped up and stamped the head of his assailant to a pulp. Now he had nothing to lose.

Back on his feet he ran through the entrance and bounced his way through pushing infected aside much to their complete surprise. As he pummelled his way on he could see the roof of the surrounded range rover getting slowly closer. The horde grappled and grabbed at him as he passed but were much slower to react than himself.

His speed slowed as he neared his vehicle due to the volume of infected pressing into him. He passed the pick to his left hand and drew his pistol. He needed to clear some room so he could get in the door.

He fired rapidly ensuring clean headshots to the nearest of the infected. He had managed to clear a space two remained in his way. He pistol whipped the first out of his route. He wedged the hot barrel of the gun into the throat of the second and fired spraying the rear window with blood and shattering it simultaneously. He threw the pistol through the broken window and into the rear of the car. Grabbing the handle he yanked the door and pulled it open far enough to get in as the rabble pushed in towards him again.

The undead peered in through the windows, and arms flailed through the broken rear. They tried to scratch their way in to the warm meat within. Jumping into the driver's seat he turned the key and started the powerful V8 engine, putting it into reverse he pulled the vehicle back a few feet, then slamming it into drive he floored it, having no idea how wide the group was even from the elevated position in the driver's seat, he started by driving with the flow to lessen damage and gain ground, then as he felt the car hit the road he turned at right angles with it following the road back towards the exit. The car jolted as it ran over body after body like driving through a field of maize there was a constant thrum on the bodywork as arms, legs and bodies were flung aside.

Then all of a sudden he saw daylight ahead. The throng thinned and the laboured engine gained enough traction to move up through the automatic gearbox. Speeding up he put more distance between himself and the immense horde.

As his heart rate slowed and the weakness came on from muscles screaming with lactic acid, he slowed and then stopped the car at the crest of a rise. There were very few infected where he had halted.

He opened the sunroof and climbed to a standing position on the front seats. From his vantage point on the rise overlooking East 8 he had a perfect view of the entire site, it was decimated.

The horde of infected stretched as far as the eye could see in both directions, like a winding river of stumbling rotten flesh, East 8 was acting like a dam, causing the flow to separate and re-connect once the obstacle had been passed, like a boulder damming a white water stretch of a river. Jack was in awe, he had never seen so many of the creatures in one place. It also confirmed his fear of the infected flocking together into humongous groups. If a mass like the one here hit the lighthouse, it would become their eternal mausoleum for sure.

22 LODGINGS

Jack ripped the rear-view mirror from the windshield and looked at his savaged ear. The lower part, which included the lobe was completely missing. His neck was swamped with fresh and drying blood. He checked the rest of himself over, as the adrenalin was easing down numerous aches and pains descended on him. He located many scratches and minor lacerations on all areas of exposed flesh.

A sigh departed his lips, the killing crew would die with him. On a deeper level now he knew the information needed to survive and revive the human race, the old ways of slash and burn that the crew had adopted, would no longer be required making people like him outdated and redundant.

He leaned into the backseat. After retrieving his pistol from the foot well and reloading it, he located his first aid pack and pulled it onto the passenger seat. He flicked open the catches, Jack first located a tablet bottle marked dihydracodeine and took a couple of the strong painkillers.

He dowsed his ear and other minor wounds with neat alcohol from a small bottle in the pack. It stung like crazy but stopped the bleeding enough to apply a pad over his injury. He folded the wadding and used some surgical tape to hold it in place over the wound.

Knowing the ramifications of his injuries, it was imperative that he get back to Sarah to give her the information he held as soon as possible. Hence the need to patch up the wound fast, he knew he was dead in the long run but he needed to keep strong for as long as possible, he had to get moving. There was another job he wanted to attend to before he headed back to the lighthouse.

Jack travelled along relatively clear roads, both free of infected and vehicle blockages. The roads close to East 8 were very well travelled by scavenging parties, and were kept accessible from fairly early on in the epidemic.

He pulled the car into a familiar road. Ahead of him the row of houses where Sarah had been hiding with the girls appeared further on down the hill. He pulled up and shut off the engine at the point where he'd left the bikes on the day they had first met, back when the crew were still three.

A short way ahead his eyes fixed on the point of the verge at the reason why he had returned. He could see the corpse of Randal hadn't moved.

With heavy heart he climbed out of the range rover. He opened up the rear window and dropped the tail gate. The shovel slid out with ease and he walked over to the body.

Randal was unrecognisable apart from his clothing. The wildlife and weather had savaged any bare flesh and his body seemed to have become a haven for parasites and insect life. If it wasn't for his paramilitary garb Jack wouldn't have been able to distinguish him from the rest of the never to rise again corpses.

He started to dig on the wide verge next to the body. It was to be the last resting place of his friend.

It took him some time to get the grave deep enough to bury him to about three feet in depth, not the six foot he would have liked but it was enough to create a perfect grave. The weather was unseasonably warm and due to his injuries he was suffering badly. He rested for a moment at the rear of the car and drank some warm bottled water. He poured some into his cupped hand and washed it over his face avoiding the pad covering his ear.

He sighed heavily and proceeded to move Randal's body into the makeshift grave. First he took the corpse by the shoulders and eased his torso into the hole and then he gently lifted his legs in. He ignored the tell-tail movements of the living creatures within Randal. After straightening the body he knelt by the freshly dug plot. Although not particularly a lover of God he said a short prayer, he wasn't entirely sure what he should say but starting with our father and ending with amen seemed to be the way to go.

After a few minutes of reflection he rose and finished covering the body. He rammed the shovel into the dirt at the head leaving it as a grave marker. He closed the trunk and retook his position back behind the wheel of his four wheel drive.

The pain from his ear was ever present and distracting. He popped the lid from the pill bottle and swallowed another couple of the strong painkillers. Within seconds the warm glow he received from the pharmaceuticals relieved the injury and numbed many lesser ones.

His mind came back to his task at hand. If he was to get the information to Sarah and the girls he needed to get moving. He felt that he didn't have long, he just didn't feel right, and darkness wallowed in the back of his mind.

He started up the car and with a last admiring look to the mound of earth, the new home of one of his friends, he pulled away. He felt some remorse that he wasn't able to properly put Simon to rest, but in his eyes Simon's death was heroic as it allowed them time to get away.

The daylight was fading as he turned into the lane. Jack was tired. His mind drifted with thoughts of the old days. He contemplated on arguments and discussions of old, his children's parent teacher meetings, the birth of his first born, the night he met his wife.

They were both waiting for blind dates at the cinema and ended up leaving the foyer together after being left in the lurch. They walked over to a nearby pub and got to know each other. They chatted about work, friends, movies, music. As the night stretched on it seemed as though they had known each other for years. They clicked, and fitted together. Since they had drained their drinks Jack drifted over to the bar to get another round in. Jack was jolted and nearly lost his footing. He was confused as the jostling continued.

His eyes opened with a start, as he realised the car had left the road and the vehicle was bouncing along the verge. He fought with the steering wheel pulling it hard over to get back onto the tarmac. The car slewed sideways, jack stamped down hard on the brake pedal with both feet. The wheels locked and with a continuous screech the car finally stopped, stalled and rocked gently on the spot.

He breathed a sigh of relief. He wanted to return to the lighthouse before the sickness took over, but arriving in one piece would be more favourable. The truth was he had to rest up.

Not being too far from the pub they raided some time before he decided to head there.

The motor started up with no trouble. He put the transmission into drive and cautiously pulled away.

Within five minutes he pulled up in front of the pub with its overgrown hanging baskets. The two desiccated corpses still lay where he had finished them off. The door still closed. He got out taking with him the folder and his pistol. He pushed the folder into the waistband of his light weights and headed to the entrance pistol at the ready.

Jack moved light footed across the gravel forecourt swiftly, he operated the door handle of the pub and pushed it open. As he entered his nostrils were assaulted by the musty smell of decay. It was stronger since his last visit caused by the building being shut up for so long.

It was obvious no-one had been inside apart from himself and Sarah. He relaxed slightly and sauntered across to the bar, stepping behind it. A quick search of the shelves revealed a couple of small mixer bottles of tonic water that were surprisingly still in date. He slipped them into his expansive thigh pockets. Next to the open dust covered till, revealing a wad of decomposing bank notes and discoloured coins, he picked up a couple of pens and a bottle opener.

Just behind him was a closed door marked 'Private' which Jack guessed led up to the landlord's apartment. He needed to sleep; he knew the ramifications of resting for too long but could not continue as he was deteriorating fast. It was somewhere they had not investigated on their first visit.

The silence was broken as Jack banged on the door a few times with the barrel of his Glock. Then he put his ear close to the door, listening intently. It wasn't long before he heard the tell tail fumbling's and groans of one of the infected.

With a sigh Jack slipped the safety off on his gun and raised the farmhouse style latch on the door. He pushed it open and stepped into the short hallway. Ahead was a flight of stairs up to the next level. He moved forward carefully, gun leading the way.

The steps creaked as he mounted them. He moved up slowly keeping his gun level with just above the top step. A clearer groan issued from the landing above. Jack stopped and held position as a bulbous pale balding head came into view. He lined up the rear sight with the red enhanced foresight. With his breath held, he squeezed the trigger. The pistol bucked in his hand letting out a sharp crack which momentarily deafened him in the narrow area. The infected man dropped out of sight, its face rearranged into a surprised grimace by the entry of the bullet.

Jack got to the top of the staircase. He lowered the weapon and looked with disgust at what probably used to be the landlord. He had been a big man in life. Most likely worked out in earlier life but it seemed the muscle tone had succumbed to fat cells, and his sense of self-esteem had disappeared along with his hairline.

He stepped carefully around the corpse which pretty much blocked the entire corridor. A mixture of open and closed doors leading from either side greeted him.

The first open door was the lounge; everything was in disarray after months of the infected landlord bumbling around. The next was the kitchen, the smell of decayed food warning him long before he tentatively looked inside.

The next door he came across was closed. He opened it quickly and stepped back with his gun at the ready. Nothing attacked him. It was a small box room and contained nothing but a single bed. It was all he needed and wanted at this time.

Daylight was almost gone, replaced by long shadows. Sat on the bed he took the items he'd scavenged from his pockets and placed them next to him on the bed. He opened one of the bottles of tonic and took a swig, then placed it on the floor at his feet.

With his small torch gritted in his teeth his picked up the file and one of the pens and wrote a short note on its cover. After he had finished he placed them on the floor and curled up in foetal position on the bed. Within seconds he had fallen asleep.

The dawn chorus brought him from his slumber. He ached from head to toe. The infection had taken root and was working hard to take him over. He remembered what Simon had said after he had been bitten. The darkness was trying to cloud his mind. He forced it back with good thoughts about his old family and what could've been his new one. He had to get back to Sarah quickly.

He struggled up to a seated position. The second bottle of water was in his hand and he fumbled with it to release its fluid. He downed the room temperature liquid in a couple of gulps. He released a booming burp as he finished and dropped the bottle on the floor with its partner.

Standing up he swayed for a moment then regained his steadiness a little. He secured the folder back in his belt at his back and gathered up the rest of his belongings stowing them in appropriate pockets.

He stumbled slightly to the door. He pulled down the handle and opened it wide.

The infected woman was on him in a heartbeat. Jack, taken totally by surprise, flailed and dropped his Glock. He descended backwards with the blond woman's weight knocking him off balance. She reminded him of another woman, a workmate who died in his arms early on when this conflict started. He landed hard on his back the woman's snapping teeth mere inches from his face, infected spittle spraying him. She was so close her fetid rotten breath made him retch.

She clawed at his face and neck, pulling clear the bandage that covered his previously infected wound. In panic Jack scrabbled around trying to get purchase to push her off. The two glass bottles clinked together as they were knocked aside.

Jack was finally getting the upper hand. He pushed her back by the neck with one hand, with the other he grabbed for one of the bottles. He managed to push her back to arm's length and then he smashed the bottle with a punch into the woman's open mouth. The momentum launched her away from him, making her land on her back in the doorway.

Shooting his head left and right he caught a glimpse of his gun by the wall. He plucked it up and turned it towards his assailant. Just as her head rose he fired instantly coating a cone shaped layer of brain matter and skull fragments across the carpet of the hallway.

Using the bed for purchase, Jack pulled himself up. He inspected the corpse in front of him. Her nametag read 'You have been served by Andrea'. He scoffed a laugh.

'No tip today, Andrea.' He said as he stepped over her and moved on into the hallway. Despite the pain from the old and new injuries he edged past the heavy set corpse and down the stairs. He stumbled out of the pub. A few infected were heading in his direction, possibly lured by the gunshot. He no longer cared and continued to limp over to the car.

Once inside he located the first aid kit and dry swallowed a few more of the painkillers from it. He sat back allowing a couple of minutes for the drugs to kick in. He stared through the windscreen at the few infected that were heading towards him. He didn't want to end up like them, he hated them. He turned the key starting the engine. Clicking the lever into drive he stamped down on the accelerator. Gravel threw up from all four wheels, keeping the steering wheel straight he ploughed straight through the small horde in front of him.

He continued to drive quickly knowing that his time was short. But before he turned he still had one job left to do. He must get the information to Sarah.

23 ARRIVAL

She lay awake and heard the door to the lighthouse clang shut, Jack's kiss still on her lips. He had gone to do his detective work. She didn't want him to go, but understood his reasons. They had all lost a great deal because of this epidemic, some more than others. Sarah at least still had her children whereas Jack had seen his wife and his children become infected, in effect he had lost everything. He just wanted to know why, and how to fix it.

Sarah quietly slipped out of bed and climbed up to the lamp room. Jack was already halfway up the staircase to the carpark. She picked up the binoculars winding until his figure came into focus. 'Don't go.' She whispered under her breath biting her bottom lip. But he continued to walk on towards the gate. As he unlocked it and finally disappeared from view she lowered the binoculars.

Jack had made sure they were well stocked with fresh food from the allotments before he left. But the time would eventually come when she would have to leave the comfort of the lighthouse and restock on essentials herself if he didn't return.

The girls were now much more secure but she still never wanted them too far away from her, apart from her jaunts up the steps, but she made sure they were safe inside on those occasions. She hadn't left them alone for long ever since the day she had killed her husband. After she had done it she sat in the closet staring at his body and crying for a further thirty minutes or so.

When she had composed herself a little she had gone through to her daughters' room and coaxed the two semi catatonic girls out of the wardrobe. After a few days of being locked in, their food was just about run out. She packed the girls and a few meagre possessions into her car and left. There was no plan as to where they were going, she just drove.

The car was attacked by people on many occasions. They also witnessed accidents and rioting. They managed to get stuck at one point, the car entirely surrounded by infected people. The girls we screaming as the people slapped and banged all around on the windows and bodywork.

Eventually a military group came along and cleared the horde, rescuing them from the ruined car and bundling them into the back of a lorry. The soldiers were good to them and after feeding them, they escorted all three to the refugee camp.

Every morning and evening she walked down to the outcrop and sat for a while watching the car park beyond the gate, in the hope that Jack would drive in and greet her with a warm embrace. Extreme situations were notorious for creating close relationships. She knew it from her previous police training but it didn't stop her having feelings for him. Despite thinking herself as a modern independent woman she still felt she needed someone, needed Jack.

On the fourth morning after Jack had left she rose early. She slowly slipped out from under the covers and off the bed so as not to disturb the sleeping children. The cool air of the room wrapped around her exposed legs and arms making her shiver. She pulled on a pair of denims and sweatshirt. With a glance back at the girls still peacefully sleeping she mounted the steps up to the lens room.

It was shaping up to be a clear day and visibility all round was perfect. Sarah sat in Jacks chair as she did quite a great deal; it helped her feel closer to him. She looked out taking in the impressive view all around.

She took in the breath taking view of the horizon and the rising sun heralding the new day. Looking out to sea made it hard to believe the world had collapsed. There were no wrecked buildings, rusting cars or overgrown plants. More importantly there were none of the infected ghouls.

Sarah moved around and looked inland towards the carpark she could just make out the gate in the middle distance. Something caught her eye. It looked like the shadow of a figure at the gate. She snatched up the binoculars from the sill that ran full circle around the room. She brought them up to her eyes and spun the wheel on top to bring them into sharper focus on the access to the stairway. There was definitely a figure up against the gate.

Jack? She put down the binoculars and quietly she jogged down the stairs.

'Mummy?'

'Hey Charlotte. Good morning sweetheart.' She said as she leant against the bedhead and pulled on her trainers.

'I'm just going to the gate. I won't be long, okay?'

'Okay. Is Jack back?' She replied groggily and lay back down.

'Let's hope so sweetheart.'

Sarah smiled and climbed down to the lower level. She reached up to the top cupboard and retrieved the Sig Sauer Jack had given her back at the house they had found them in. She checked the mag and noting it was full she slammed it back in the grip and slid the slide back to chamber a round.

She left the lighthouse pulling the door closed behind her. After double checking the door was closed properly she started to briskly walk up the steps to the car-park.

In anticipation the journey was faster than normal; she slowed as she approached the gate. Something wasn't right, the figure had the build of Jack but something just wasn't right. Her mouth gaped in horror as she realised the figure behind the gate really was Jack, a very dead Jack.

She stood transfixed, the dead milky eyes stared back at her imploringly, and as she stood there the cadaver of her once good friend, saviour and possibly future lover, raised his arm through the railings holding something out seemingly towards her. It couldn't be, these infected just wanted to attack. It's as if Jack was actually aware of himself, even after death.

She moved forward tentatively. Jack held his arm at full stretch. It was holding a file, she tentatively stretched out and took hold of it, Jack immediately let go and pulled his arm back through the fence. Sarah stepped back and looked at the tatty folder she now held then back at Jack. She opened the folder and briefly flicked through it. The words meant nothing at the present time. She turned the folder over and noticed a hand-written note on the back. She looked back at Jack slightly perplexed. She then read what was written on the back.

'Sarah, if you're reading this I have succeeded in getting this important information to you, there is a future. Your daughters are part of the next generation there's nothing more important than them. Get them to safety. With all my love. Jack. PS, shoot me, but never regret it'

Sarah looked sympathetically at the zombie in front of her, tears welling in her eyes. She couldn't shoot him, he got this far and she assumed some part of him must still be left. But then his mouth opened into a snarl and he began to push at the gate as if trying to get through, he was just another victim of the Isaiah effect.

As the sun rose higher in the sky the peacefulness was briefly shattered by the sharp crack of a single gunshot. After a flock of birds flew off from a nearby tree disturbed by the sound, the silence of the new day returned.

24 TRUTH

By lunchtime Sarah knew the truth about the current state of the World. She had sat in the lens room studying the file all morning while the girls played quietly downstairs. Earlier that day she had despatched Jack with a bullet to the brain. It was a difficult task, but had turned out for the best. He was gone long before he had got back to them. She couldn't believe that he had actually managed to return despite having passed over; if that's how you could describe it nowadays.

The contents of the folder had made everything clear, and it had also given her hope of a new life for them.

The virus that started the pandemic was an amalgamation of a biological weapon that had evolved with the help of pollution and the lack of immunity within modern man. That made sense to Sarah. Antibiotics losing their potency with continued use being the biggest example.

The original virus originated from the Ukraine and had pushed outwards into Russia and Europe as a result of a hushed up accident at the plant it was produced in. The heaviest of populated areas, such as cities succumbed faster than the countryside. It was Worldwide with virtually no areas of the globe that remained unscathed. The United Kingdom fared much better with the natural defence of being an island to its advantage. It was possible that there were other places remaining uninfected, but as worldwide communications died it was unable to be proven.

Initial thoughts that the infection was a terrorist attack were unfounded. Further research by the American government discovered the condition was actually genetic and only exacerbated by the virus. This meant, and was proven, that the original anti-virus just didn't work on the evolving version. The Christian right fell on this fact and it was labelled as gods design, aka the rapture. The government named it the Isaiah effect, after a verse from the bible. Isaiah chapter twenty six verse nineteen.

Everyone carried the code. There were no exceptions, no-one was immune, in death reanimation occurred. The original virus just speeded things up. When bitten or scratched by anyone infected or one of the reanimated, the pre-conditioned genetic code is activated causing the Isaiah effect.

Currently only roughly five percent of the population of the United Kingdom remained. But again due to lack of communication it was merely an estimate.

Mankind was fighting back. They managed to save Scotland. It was a safe zone with humans numbering around two point eight million and walkers zero. Due to the size of the landlocked country and it's relatively low population in the first place it was easier to keep control. Especially as Hadrian's Wall had been reinstated and was continually patrolled.

There were estimates that a further one hundred thousand people were in twenty five camps all down the east side of the country, and a few hundred renegade survivalists' were fending for themselves. But these figures were severely out of date as one of the camps listed was the one herself and the girls had been at until it was destroyed.

Deliveries of supplies had suspended due to a serious onslaught on the border by an immense horde of undead a few months earlier. The numbers of the horde were immeasurable but had been estimated in the hundreds of thousands. Sarah couldn't comprehend a mass of infected that large. They would have cut through the border like a lawnmower cutting grass. With the added facility of eating everyone they came across.

With the use of heavy firepower and light air support the living won the fight. There were heavy casualties but the people over the border were protected, and the undead were deflected back into the wastelands of England.

The supply chain was simple. Essential items were shipped from the safe zone on a bi-weekly basis. Gas rigs out in the North Sea were kept stocked up by ship and items were relayed to the camps with the use of Bell 206 helicopters, one of which every rig had. The rigs were manned all year round and had a constant presence for observation of the mainland and organisation of the supply drops.

Sadly there was no indication why the supply drops had not recommenced. Unless of course, there was no point as all the camps were gone.

She looked up from the paperwork and was already formulating a plan. Within the file was a list of the relay rigs and a nautical map of their positions, the nearest being a mere twenty miles from their current position.

She had no problem reading both map and compass, and Jack had already prepared the marine dinghy which would be perfect to get them to the rig.

They left the lighthouse and started to walk up the steps towards the car park. Sarah led carrying a shovel and the girls followed dutifully hand in hand. She owed it to Jack to put him to rest properly.

When she had reached the gate she could see his body still laid out where he had previously fallen.

'You stay on this side girl's,' she said turning back to them.

'Okay mummy,' they replied almost in unison.

After closing the gate she stood for a few moments looking at the ravaged body of Jack. She felt sorrow and regret for what they could have had. She unclasped the utility belt that he wore and rolled him off it.

'Is he going to wake up, mummy?' said Charlotte from the opposite side of the fence, a concerned look on both the girls faces.

'No dear he won't,' she replied reassuringly.

Finding some soft sandy soil close by, she dug a shallow grave to lay him in. His body was lighter than expected and she managed to roll him in with little effort.

She took a last longing look at him before covering him with earth. Leaning on the shovel she lingered over the makeshift grave.

'Mummy, are those his friends?' said Charlotte.

Sarah looked in the direction which her daughter was pointing. Through the neat row of cars numerous infected came stumbling out towards her.

'Uh oh, bad people,' came Sally's voice as she threw the shovel over the fence and fumbled with the gate. The group headed ever closer.

Sarah suddenly remembered the utility belt lying close to the grave. She turned back and made a grab for it, just as one of the infected got hold of the opposite end. In a macabre tug of war Sarah dragged the beast with her towards the gate.

Eventually the weak rotten fingers could hold on no more. The buckle slipped pulling the rotten flesh from its hand like a glove being removed. Sarah fell sideways close to the gate the resistance now gone.

The horde was almost upon her as she scrabbled to her feet. The screams of the girls on the other side of the fence spurred her on. She quickly pulled the ice axe from the belt and gripped it by the handle. She swung the axe embedding the point in the side of the tugging losers head.

After recovering the pick she forced her way through the gate. With no time to secure it she threw the belt over her shoulder, plucked Sally up with one hand and gripped Charlotte's wrist with the other. They hurried down towards the lighthouse.

'Pyewacket.' Sally cried out. Sarah looked back to see the stuffed animal lying atop a step just a few feet behind them. She let go of Charlottes wrist briefly and deftly plucked it up giving it back to Sally.

The horde was still a long way back, but they were making ground heading down the staircase in an unruly crowd towards them. Sarah headed straight past the lighthouse and on to the boathouse.

Their time on Earth was finished, well for the current generation. The future of the human race was in the hands of the next generation. The Isaiah effect would eventually burn itself out, although the re-animation would continue, but that is easily remedied. Hopefully they wouldn't make the same mistakes this time round. And from her husband and Jack, Sarah had inherited the strength to protect her daughters and ensure their safety as they grew. Eventually they would become strong enough to fend for themselves.

Standing and steering the boat with one hand she stared back at the lighthouse as if expecting to see the spirit of Jack watching over them. Turning back to face the wind and spray she caressed the ice axe holstered in the utility belt that she wore around her waist.

She realised her fight was not quite over, but she had the strength and impetus to strive for a future for mankind. She would never give up while she still had breath in her body.

25 RIG

The lighthouse was out of sight within twenty minutes. The sea was being kind, not a millpond but not very choppy. The air was fresh, Sarah realised that the mainland was rotten, the smell was always present you just got used to it. It wasn't until she was away from it that she noticed.

She grew concerned. Now the land was out of sight it was impossible to keep on a stable heading. She piloted by compass keeping on course towards the rig where she estimated it to be. The girls sat together, eyes squinting with the wind and spray. Their orange lifejackets making them look twice as wide.

'What's that mummy?' said Charlotte pointing off to the left.

On the horizon the red intertwined metalwork of the rig came into view.

'Well done girlie. You've spotted where we're headed' she answered with a smile and steered the boat over to put it dead on course.

As they approached the sheer size of the structure became evident. The platform was suspended a good hundred feet above the surface supported by four wide steel columns intertwined with a lattice of steelwork. To one side was attached what looked like a four storey tower block, presumably quarters, offices and canteen for the workers. Opposite the block the derrick rose a further fifty feet above.

She headed towards a small docking pontoon attached between two of the legs at sea level. The rig itself looked deserted. Sarah eased off the throttle and turned the boat almost side on as she prepared to dock. She closed off the throttle totally and picked up the mooring rope. Deftly she stepped onto the gently undulating platform and tied the boat up.

Still no-one came to greet them. Sarah was worried. She helped the girls to get off the dingy.

'Now girls, we're going to head up to the main deck,' she said motioning to the narrow staircase to the side of the platform. 'We're going to hold hands with me in the front. Okay?'

Her daughters nodded in unison. She led them tentatively up the steps. Sarah noticed that the rig was in poor state of repair, paint flaked from the metalwork everywhere. With nearly a year of being exposed to the elements and no maintenance crews she wasn't surprised. As they reached the main deck Sarah noticed that the walkways and stairs were far smaller than she imagine, there was barely room for two people to pass. She imagined it must have been claustrophobic for the workers, ironic considering the open ocean around them.

She halted before they reached the quarters block. The steel door was hanging open.

'You two wait here, hold onto the railing and I'll be back in a jiffy.' she almost whispered to them.

'Mummy, I'm scared.' Charlotte returned.

Sarah knelt in front of her daughter.

'Don't worry, I'm just going to look through the doorway.'

She pulled the pistol from its holster and smiled back towards the girls as she entered the dark interior. The darkness was only in the doorway, as she trained her gun along the corridor fluorescent tubes lit its full length. She took a step back to the doorway and beckoned the girls inside.

They headed along the corridor. A large green arrow pointed them in the direction of the operations room. They approached a Tee junction. As Sarah drew level she glanced down it then froze, the girls hand in hand almost walked into her.

Not ten feet in front of her stood a man. He walked towards her briskly. Unsure she raised the gun at the ready. His face came out of the shadows. His eyes were milky white. Sarah fired. The bullet ripped into the man's shoulder knocking him off kilter for a split second. Before she could let off a second round the man collided with her she flew back into the wall. The girls screamed hysterically. Sarah was dazed. She scrabbled to her feet to see the Isaiah victim disappear out of the door they came in. Sally was huddled against the wall tightly clutching Pyewacket and sobbing.

'Where's Charlotte, no please no.' Sarah screamed. 'Stay there.' She stammered to sally and then ran towards the door.

Tears streamed down her face as she exited into the daylight. The screaming pinpointed her destination. Her footfalls rang out as she ran around the walkway. Then she saw him, he had Charlotte up against the railing near the helipad.

'Leave my daughter alone,' she howled.

She raised the gun and fired whilst still on the run releasing three rounds, the first hit him square in the back, the second missed and the third caught him in the head. He tipped forward onto the rail. His centre of gravity shifted and he went over. Sarah just reached them too late as the man's weight took Charlotte over the edge with him.

She watched with open mouthed terror as both figures disappeared beneath the waves never to resurface.

Sarah's heart was ripped out, she knelt in shock. Her stare fixed on the point a hundred feet below where the ocean had just swallowed up her eldest daughter.

She barely registered Sally nuzzle up to her repeating 'Where's Charlie, Mummy, where's Charlie?'

She also didn't hear the whoop whoop of the helicopter blades, or the downdraft as it touched down on the helipad. She was pretty much catatonic as the pilot strapped her into one of the rear seats of the Bell Jet next to Sally.

One and a half hours later, they touched down in Scotland.

26 NORTH

It had been two years since Sarah and Sally had been brought to safety. It took Sarah some weeks to come to terms with the loss of Charlotte. It was something that would stay with her for the rest of her life. She wasn't alone none of the several hundred survivors in the small highland coastal town were unscarred by the Isaiah effect. Everybody had lost something and someone, many had lost everything.

Scotland had had its problems with the Isaiah effect. The town they now resided in was a ghost town before the survivors revitalised it. The country was easy to clear not having the density of population like England.

Despite the town being comfortable and safe, the way in which people traded had changed considerably. Bartering was the key. The only supermarket in town now resembled a flea market every morning. People would take produce and swap for different items. Lawns no longer existed as fertile land was at a premium. All gardens became vegetable plots. Animals such as chickens and goats roamed everywhere.

The townsfolk came from many areas of life, mostly people with skills. John, a friend of Sarah's, had a theory.

'You know why only useful people survived?' he had said. 'Because the useless layabouts waited for someone else to do something like they always do.'

He worked with Sarah as part of the lookout team. John had been a builder in London when it had all started. Although Sarah thought he looked more like some sort of archetypal criminal. Initially he viewed her as an enemy, but as time passed they became friends. He had told her how he and another guy had been the only people to escape a building site that was attacked by a horde. They went their separate ways soon after.

John had also told her how he had drunk himself stupid for days, and partied hard to the end of the world. Eventually he was the only one left to party. Once he had straightened out and realised it really was the end unless he fought back, he headed north knowing Scotland had castles, and he wanted to live in one.

Despite his faults she was fond of John and was happy to have him at her back.

Jobs within the new society were based on skill set. Sarah was a supervisor overseeing the protection of the town based on her previous police experience. John was a lookout working under her as he was tough. They had teachers, a doctor and two nurses, plumbers, electricians, fishermen, even firemen and, of course, a helicopter pilot.

They took homes relative to their needs. Sarah, Sally and her new daughter Jackie lived together in a two bedroom cottage. It was self-contained with a well in the back garden that they shared with their neighbours. They even had hot water supplied by a back boiler behind the fireplace in the living room. Larger more opulent houses were shared by however many people could comfortably live in them. John got his castle, but did share it with another twenty single people. He still stated he was its king.

It was a picturesque place to live, despite the extreme weather conditions in winter. There were only two roads in and out of town. Tall craggy hills surrounded three sides and the sea on the other. The dock was purely for local fishermen and a ferry had connected it to nearby islands.

Further along the dockside, after the light industrial units was situated a ministry of defence facility, it was deserted early in the pandemic. What use would a nuclear submarine maintenance depot be against Isaiah?

Thankfully they left behind fuel, stores, ammunition and even a few weapons. Dennis, the helicopter pilot was the sole resident of the small base. It was perfect for his needs, especially as it had a helipad and hangar which were perfect for his five seater Bell 206 helicopter that he flew as a charter craft before Isaiah. He felt comfortable there being retired military himself.

Sarah walked away from the cottage. She stopped by the ferry port and took a deep breath of fresh morning sea air. She turned and carried on up the main street past the bank which now served no purpose whatsoever, its vault was still full of cash and valuables, neither of which were needed in the new world. Opposite that stood the long glass fronted supermarket. No-one was around at this early hour. She preferred the nightshift, but occasionally went in during the day. Working nights meant she could leave after the children went to bed and return as they woke. The neighbours were only too happy to look in on them now and again. Everyone knew everyone and the whole town worked together. There were no threats from within and all the children knew the bogeyman lived outside the barricades and not in their closets.

Sarah was happy on the whole, although she still blamed herself for the death of Charlotte. Jackie coming along helped her come to terms with the loss. It just dulled the ache enough to keep it in the background. When Doctor MacGregor first informed her she was pregnant she called him everything under the sun, accusing his equipment of being faulty then informing him he'd be up on a malpractice charge.

He was a kind man and understood her anger. It was a complete mess of a world to bring a child into. He helped her come to terms with it, and when it finally dawned on her that this child was Jacks last bequeath to the planet, she finally accepted the responsibility. Jackie was now over a year old and healthy. Every time Sarah looked into her eyes she saw Jack, it reminded her of the last time she forgot about the effect and the wrecked country, albeit for a fleeting furtive moment. The teacher and nurses were great when the need for their nursery services was required. Schooling wasn't a straightforward thing anymore. The teacher taught them reading, writing and basic math, just the essentials, and the teaching was done while the children's guardians were out doing their chores for the community.

Sarah climbed up to the platform to find John there gazing down towards the main road into town.

'Morning John.' she said.

'Alright girl?' he replied

She smiled in reply as he turned to her.

Over to their right the helicopter slowly rose above the roofs of the naval buildings.

Hovering level with the tower he raised a hand to them from inside the cabin and they reciprocated. Dennis rose up and headed south towards the border. Sarah leaned on the edge of the parapet and followed the chopper heading towards the horizon.

'Has 'e seen any sign of life lately?' said John.

Sarah looked back to him

'Nope, he's covered all the islands within fifty miles radius. He doesn't go right to the border any more, conserving fuel.'

'No bother, there's plenty of us here anyway,' he smiled.

An hour later the helicopter returned.

'He ain't been gone long,' said John with a strained face.

Sarah looked equally confused. Dennis was normally gone for three to four hours on a reconnaissance flight. The bird headed straight in towards the helipad.

'He's two up,' said John as Dennis neared the landing pad.

'I'll check it out,' said Sarah as she headed down the ladder. She made a b-line directly for the open gates of the navy compound. Once inside she walked between two of the buildings and came out close to the helipad. The rotors on the helicopter were slowly rotating down to a standstill and Dennis was outside holding open the door helping a man in green combat gear down.

'What's going on?' she asked as she approached them.

'Picked this guy up about forty miles away,' he said 'Let's get him inside and comfortable and I'll tell you the rest.'

His demeanour made Sarah very nervous.

27 VISITOR

The coffee pot was full as Sarah picked it up and filled her mug. She turned briskly and sat at the table in the small canteen. Dennis walked in through the double doors and made himself a coffee adding three spoons of sugar.

'Take it easy on the sugar there's hardly any left.' She said
'Somehow I don't think we'll need it,' he replied.
'Pardon?'
'I don't think we'll be here much longer, there's a massive horde on its way.'

Sarah choked spitting coffee onto the table. Dennis never did beat around the bush.

'The man I brought in is infected. I've sedated him and locked him in one of the holding cells. He's comfortable.' He continued 'I headed out past the castle following the main road. As I approached Loch Neil I saw them, the biggest horde I've ever seen it stretched as far as I could see.'

'My God, what about the man?' she asked.
'They were following him, thankfully he was far enough ahead for me to drop down and pluck him up.'
'How long do you think he has?' Sarah asked.
'A few hours, tops,' he said nonchalantly. 'He only has minor scratches.'
'We better ask him some questions then,' she said.

Dennis agreed, drained his coffee and stood up. He lifted his jacket and took his Glock out of his shoulder holster, checked it, then returned it out of sight.

'I'll deal with him once we have the answers.'

They left the canteen and headed deeper into the small compound. They quickly reached a door with a military police sign attached. The small office acted as a central hub for the authorities that made sure the navy boys followed the rules.

To one side a short corridor led to two interview rooms. On the end wall was a secure room, the electronic pad had been removed. Inside were weapons and ammunition, a mixture of military, police and hunting guns. This was the community's armoury. The last door led to the holding cells. There were 4 in total, staggered in two pairs on either side of the hallway.

Dennis motioned Sarah ahead towards the first cell. He handed her a bottle of water. She looked in through the small reinforced glass window in the door at the bedraggled looking soldier. He was sat up on the bench leaning against the wall. His eyes flicked open at the sound of the keys jangling in the lock.

'Hello, I'm Sarah,' she said as she handed the bottle to him and sat down.

'Clean water? Thank you,' he replied as he struggled to undo the cap with grubby tired fingers. He raised it to his mouth with a shaking hand and guzzled the liquid greedily. His face was unshaven and raked in places with a rawness caused by fingernails. He noticed Sarah looking at him.

'If you're wondering, yes, the infected did this. I know I'm finished,' he said calmly. 'Not that it's important, but my names Jamie.'

'Where have you come from? We haven't seen anyone else around here for nearly a year.'

'Hadrian's Wall,' he said.

Dennis gasped. 'My god, I've not been as far as the barricade for months, please tell me it hasn't fallen.'

'It fell weeks ago, we retreated to Glasgow but they followed, there were millions of them. They smothered us like a blanket.' A tear made a track through the grime on his cheek as he remembered.

'Are you telling us you walked from Glasgow? That's a good couple of hundred miles away,' said Sarah.

'Wow, didn't realise I walked that far. I was just trying to keep ahead of them,' Jamie said.

Sarah turned and looked at Dennis 'How far away are they?' she said to him.

'Forty miles at the most,'

'We have to evacuate,' said Sarah as she stood and headed for the door. 'We'll try and make you comfortable Jamie. You have to understand we can't take you with us.'

His head drooped, 'Yes I understand.'

'I'll fix you up a good meal, I bet you're hungry,' said Dennis.

Jamie looked up and managed a weak smile. 'That would be great, thanks.'

Sarah left Jamie with Dennis. She went back to the tower.

'What's the score?' said John as she met him on the platform.

'The guy was from Hadrian's Wall, its fallen, and there's a massive horde on its way.'

'Oh,' he said showing no surprise 're having company.'

A few hours later most of the inhabitants of the town were gathered in the supermarket. The building not only served as a trading post but, because it was the biggest open area within the town, also as a meeting house.

Sarah had briefed the town council earlier on. They were now all sat at the end of the room. Dennis was still looking after their new visitor, while John was keeping watch at the tower.

'Can we have some order please?' the spokesman of the council shouted. A hush from the previous mumbles and grumbles fell over the room and all eyes looked expectantly towards the low stage.

'Sadly we have some potentially disastrous news. You all know Sarah. I'm going to hand the floor over to her to explain.'

She stepped forward slightly nervous.

'As you all probably know earlier today Dennis picked up a survivor' a short ripple spread through the crowd then silence returned as Sarah continued.

'What you might not have heard yet is that the man rescued was formally a guard at our last defensive line, Hadrian's Wall. I regret to inform you all that the wall has fallen, as has Glasgow.'

Gasps went around the stunned audience.

'We were all aware that this day might eventually come. There is a large horde on its way and we have been left with no option but to evacuate the town for the time being.'

Crying was evident all around and some even broke down. After over a year f no contact with Isaiah some found it hard to come to terms with the fact it was going to be in their faces again.

'Look, I'm sorry it's the worst news but now it's time to be proactive. I'll now hand you back to the speaker who will go through the details of the relocation.'

Sarah left the floor, happy to hand it over to the counsellor. She worked her way through the sombre crowd towards the entrance. A sound from outside made her stop dead in her tracks. A bell was ringing outside, the bell.

She sped up and left the store. People were starting to panic as the bell being heard was passed on into the rest of the crowd. It had never been heard before as it was the bell they used to warn of an impending problem.

Sarah ran across the road and headed towards the tower, the source of the clanging. John stopped ringing as Sarah climbed up onto the platform.

'What's going on?' she asked.

John cast his thumb over his shoulder, a stern look on his face. Sarah followed his motioning and looked past him along the main road heading out of town.

Her mouth dropped open. Their line of vision stretched for very nearly a mile. The horde of Isaiah's was well in sight, no more than half a mile away. They were enveloping all the land as far as the eye could see.

28 HORDE

'It's too soon to lock down the town, we're just going to have to evacuate right now,' said Sarah. 'Get to the boats and make sure they're ready to load up and ship out.'

'No problem, meet you back at the chopper?' he said as he began to climb down, shouldering his assault rifle slung over his shoulder.

'Yes, we might as well do the evac as planned.'

Sarah followed him down the ladder. As John headed towards the dock Sarah went back into town in the direction of the supermarket. People were leaving the meeting place and scattering in all directions. She jogged closer to the shop.

'Get to the boats, get to the boats now,' she shouted to te other survivors.

Word passed throughout the crowd, people understood, the majority turned immediately and ran towards the dockside. Some carried on in other directions to collect their family members or friends that hadn't attended the meeting.

The evacuation plan was a simple one. It had been drawn up early in the towns creation, or re-creation. In the event of the Isaiah victims actually reaching the town, the population would lock down their houses and then take the boats to one of the nearby islands. One in particular had already been prepared with supplies and shelter.

It was less than a mile away and easy to observe the town from. The jagged cliffs and deep water was the perfect protection from attack. Then hopefully, once the Isaiah's had moved on they could re-inhabit the town again. The eventual goal was to take the country back. The corpses would eventually rot down to nothing, so in theory they should die off.

Sarah kept running. She turned the corner moving alongside a low hedge until she reached a gate. She vaulted it then ran up the asphalt path which led round to the rear of the cottage to its back door.

She barged through it in haste and skidded to a halt in the large kitchen area. Rose was one of the towns' nurses. She had been babysitting Sally and Jackie that particular day. Sarah's sudden appearance crashing through the back door and breathing heavily into the kitchen made her yelp in surprise.

'Mummy,' shouted Sally as she looked up from her colouring book on the large round kitchen table. Jackie smiled broadly from her high chair at here mothers entrance.

'What's wrong?' said Rose seeing the serious look on Sarah's face. She walked around the table.

'Rose, you have to go to the boats,' she said soothingly.

'What? I heard they were coming, but…'

'They're here already, you must go to the boats right now,' she took a breath. 'Please can you take my girls too.'

Rose whispered. 'But you're coming too surely?'

'I'll be taking up the rear with John and Dennis in the helicopter. It's part of the plan, we make sure the town is clear then leave at the last minute.'

'I want to stay with you mummy,' whined Sally.

Sarah knelt closer to her daughter.

'No dear, you have to go with Rose, you must look after your little sister,' she said.

'But mummy,' tears ran down her cheek.

'Oh sweetheart you're breaking my heart, I won't be far behind.'

Rose dressed Jackie in warm clothes while Sarah helped Sally dress and pack more clothing and a few toys into a backpack. They headed outside. A few people still hurried past, all heading in the same direction towards the docks. As they approach they can see the crowds are much bigger. Quickly they are all piling onto the three fishing boats and the ferry that were moored up. Their diesel engines were already warming up and almost ready for the off.

Sarah could see John at the front helping some of the younger residents onto the deck. They caught each other's eyes. John waved her over towards him. Sarah led Rose and the girl's around the outside of the boarding passengers towards him.

'Have you seen Dennis?' he said.

'Not since earlier, I thought he'd be here,' she replied.

She turned to her daughters and their guardian.

'Please look after them,' she pleaded with Rose.

'Of course I will, we'll meet you on the island,' she replied.

She kissed Jackie who was held in Rose's arms. Then she bent slightly to kiss Sally, as she hugged her she whispered, 'I love you.'

'I love you too mummy,' she said.

They were helped onto the deck of the packed fishing boat. They were the last aboard, crewmen released the mooring chains and all four boats were piloted out into the main channel. Sarah waved, and watched as the girls waved back.

Standing alone on the dock, John touched her shoulder,

'I know you're going to miss them, but I think it might be time to go to work.'

They left the dock and headed quickly towards the steel gates separating the town from the rest of the country. They were shaking under the pressure of the Isaiah's pounding on the other side.

'Oh shit, they're here,' said John

'Time to get airborne I think, where's that damn pilot?'

They hurried through the compound gates. John rushed off to the side to close them in an effort to buy them a little more time if the primary gates failed. Sarah headed for the entrance to the main building. The door was unlocked. She checked room after room, but she still couldn't find Dennis.

All of a sudden a twinge of realisation made her stop. Jamie the survivor Dennis had picked up. She headed towards the holding cells. She entered the foyer just as Dennis stumbled into it from the opposite side. Jamie following grabbed hold of the pilot at her appearance and pushed a pistol into his jowl so she could clearly see.

'You stay where you are, you bitch,' he spat.

Sarah froze.

'You were going to leave me here. Well now you're going to stay here and this guy's flying me out,' he said.

'I'll die first,' said Dennis through tight lips.

Sarah switched into negotiator mode. She moved her arms away from her belt and weaponry, and opened her hands in a gesture of submission.

'Come on Jamie, no-one wants this,' she said softly as she backed up to the door way.

'No, you don't, you just want me to stay here and become lunch for those things outside while you guys live like kings in safety,' he shouted.

'You're infected, we can't risk having you infect the others,' she said still calm.

'I don't give a shit about anyone else.'

'You don't say,' said Dennis the gun still pushed into his cheek.

'Now get out of my way, he's flying me out of here.'

Sarah backed up slowly through the doorway into the corridor hands still out showing her obedience.

'You know you're not going to get away,' said Sarah becoming more threatening.

'Oh yeah, you and who's army are going to stop me?' he gloated.

'No army,' she said as she turned her back.

'Just me,' said John as he stepped from his hiding place to the side of the doorway, having come in and heard the parlez a couple of minutes earlier. He pulled Jamie's gun hand away from Dennis, which allowed the pilot to get out of the way as John ploughed into him punching repeatedly.

John shook his hand and turned away from the unconscious soldier.

'I was just coming to get you both, the main gates fallen. We really ought to think about getting up,' he said pointing to the ceiling.

They left the unconscious soldier where he lay and exited the building. They stopped as they walked into the open air. The sound of the Isaiah's lust for them was overwhelming. The main gate to the settlement was gone replaced by an all-consuming solid tide of infected.

The gates to the compound shook and bowed at the sheer volume.

'Here we go again,' said John as they took to their heels and ran to the waiting helicopter only tens of yards away.

All of a sudden there was the report of a gun from behind. Sarah wheeled round mid run to see John pitch over and land heavily on the ground. Behind him, leaning against the doorway of the MOD entrance, stood Jamie smoking pistol in his hand and blood streaming down his face from a broken nose.

'You're all dead, if I'm dead you all are too,' he shouted.

Sarah looked towards John. He looked up at her he mouthed the words 'Go, now.'

She turned and ran for the chopper. Dennis was already there and the whining of the initializing jet engine blocked out the moans of the Isaiah's. Shots rang out as she pulled open the canopy door. She looked back whilst fastening her seatbelt to see John suddenly jump up in front of the advancing soldier.

The secondary gate fell and the Isaiah's piled in.

'We gotta go,' shouted Dennis over the whine of the rotors.

Bullets skimmed the metalwork and thudded into it. Sarah looked back as the helicopter gained height. John was looking up at her whilst pounding the soldiers head repeatedly onto the ground. From the ever increasing distance between them she could still make out his smile. He waved his blood soaked hand in a goodbye gesture then was gone under of wave of Isaiah infected people.

'Oh shit!' said Dennis.

'What, what?' shouted Sarah just as the dashboard lit up with red warning lights and a buzzer sounded continuously. The engine spluttered as Dennis struggled to keep control of the column.

'Fuel lines ruptured, the little shit hit us,' said Dennis as he strained and fought with the dying chopper. Black smoke issued from the engines exhaust as the machine tried to go into a spin, they were still low and the tide of Isaiah's carpeted the entire area as far as the eye could see.

With a metal clang and ensuing crunch the tail spun and decimated the top of the guard tower.

'We're going down,' shouted Dennis.

Sarah closed her eyes, and said 'I love you Sally, I love you Jackie.'

The boats were safe. They were motoring up the centre of the mile wide channel. It was a rare clear day as they headed towards the pre-prepared safe island.

Rose sat on the bow of the boat with an arm around Sally and Jackie sat in her lap. The mood among all the refugees was sombre.

Then they saw a ball of flame rise up within a black smoke cloud from the direction of their town.

Rose gasped as the crack and rumble of the explosion reached them. Tears began to run down Rose's cheeks and she gripped the girls tighter.

'Mummy?' Sally said quietly as she began to cry.

29 LATER

The sky was overcast bathing a grey iridescence over the desolate barren land. It had been over twelve years since the Isaiah effect cut through the world's population like a scythe, killing then reanimating billions of people.

Two figures wandered across the furrowed and weed strewn expanse that used to be an award winning sports complex. The bleachers were nothing more than a pile of rotten wood and rusting metal from years without repair. As the couple passed it by, the smaller of the two figures tugged at the cuff of the older ones heavy coat.

'I need a pee,' the little girl said in a quiet voice.

They stopped walking and the woman looked all around like a cat checking around for danger whilst looking after her litter. She then looked down at the girl and smiled.

'Okay, it's safe here,' she said.

While the child relieved herself the woman continued to be ever watchful. In the distance a silhouetted figure stumbled along between the immovable vehicles long since abandoned on the main road.

'Quickly now, one of them is close,' she said

The girl looked up slightly startled and quickly pulled up her two pairs of trousers. She moved over to her elder sister and clung to her side.

'Don't worry dear, its only one. Stay close and remember to watch my back,' she smiled.

The woman pulled a well looked after extendable baton from under her coat. She picked up pace heading straight for the awkwardly moving infected corpse. The child stayed a few feet behind in a formation that had become natural to her because of the amount of times they used it. The dead man turned his head then changed direction with the promise of fresh meat. He found a gap between a rusting station wagon and a van with a tree seedling winding its way from under the sun bleached bonnet and out through the radiator grill.

The woman turned sideways on flicking the baton out to full length behind her. As the gap closed between them, and the man left the cracked tarmac and entered the field, the woman broke into a run. When she was within feet she jumped up to the side bringing the weapon down hard across the side of the man's head. The momentum knocked him down into the mud where his bottom jaw hung loose on the floor. It was totally dislocated by the heavy blow and flapped uselessly as it tried to regain its feet.

Standing over him she brought the cosh down a further three times, ensuring he was despatched for good. After cleaning down the baton using the rags that hung loosely to the Isaiah victim she snapped it together and replaced it on her belt under her heavy coat.

She then took the youngsters hand and continued on their journey back to the dilapidated house they called home.

The house in which they lived was detached from other buildings, and was situated in the middle of a road. Twenty years earlier it would have been an affluent middle class area with a smart car on every drive. The woman vaguely remembered cars, but the child had never known vehicles at all, having been born screaming to a dark world of destruction and rot.

The upper floors were unusable as the roof had fallen in over most of the house. The ceilings below had been reinforced over the years to prevent any further collapse. The couple lived in what used to be the expansive living room which stretched from the front to the rear of the house. The windows and doors were padded out with timber and doors scavenged from neighbouring properties. The rear garden was totally enclosed which allowed them to keep that window uncovered.

They were the only living people for at least a twenty mile radius from the house. Mankind had become a solitary race, preferring to keep themselves to themselves. Government was gone, there was no authority. It was purely a hand to mouth existence.

When people did come across each other they usually kept a wide berth, the fear of Isaiah still strong and instinctive. The world had reverted to a meagre existence not dissimilar to medieval times.

The woman reached up high and released the locking mechanism holding the door closed. It opened with a creak and she led the girl inside, checking behind her as she shut the door behind them. She then lifted a heavy wooden joist up and dropped it into place behind the door reinforcing it.

'Time to make something to eat I think,' said the woman. The little girl beamed and the elder opened her backpack and removed all manner of fresh vegetables that they had harvested that day from untrained plots in the area.

'Go pick a tin,' she said to the girl.

She walked over to the bookcase as the woman made ready some of the vegetables. The shelves were piled high with all manner of tins and cans, some battered, some rusty, some with labels and some without.

'Mystery tin today,' she said as she handed over the unidentifiable can, its label long since gone.

'Oh goody, I like a surprise,' said the woman happily. She piled kindling and wood into the stove set in the corner of the room. She then used a tinderbox to light some wood chippings to get the fire going.

An hour later they had eaten their boiled potatoes, carrots and peach slices. The woman then rinsed the battered enamel plates in the water butt outside the rear window. The girl dried them with a grubby towel and left them on the window sill ready for their next meal.

Darkness fell as the couple made themselves comfortable on masses of pillows and cushions in front of the glowing embers of the stove.

'Time to sleep I think,' said the woman.

'I'm tired,' replied the girl almost asleep already. As they cuddled together the woman reached back picking an item from a nearby tatty coffee table.

'You might want this,' she said as she passed the hairless cuddly toy over to the child.

'Pyewacket!' she exclaimed with a smile and wide eyes.

'Always look after him. I hope you love him as much as I did when I was your age,' said Sally to her sister.

ABOUT THE AUTHOR

Paul S Huggins hails from the United Kingdom within the witchcraft rich county of Suffolk, and resides there with his Wife, two daughters and a familiar. His introduction to the genre was being scared to death at an early age by a movie called 'Dawn of the Dead'. It changed his whole aspect on the apocalypse, and now thinks when not if! With numerous short stories published, Paul would say zombies are in his blood, but thankfully he is still living.

This is his first novel, but likely not his last.

Made in the USA
Charleston, SC
23 September 2013